A Very Fine Line

A Very Fine Line

JULIE JOHNSTON

Tundra Books

Published in Canada by Tundra Books,
75 Sherbourne Street, Toronto, Ontario M5A 2P9

Published in the United States by Tundra Books of Northern New York,
P.O. Box 1030, Plattsburgh, New York 12901

Library of Congress Control Number: 2005910621

Library and Archives Canada Cataloguing in Publication

Johnston, Julie, 1941-
    A very fine line / Julie Johnston.

ISBN-13: 978-0-88776-746-3
ISBN-10: 0-88776-746-X

    I. Title.

PS8569.O387V47 2006   jC813'.54   C2005-907313-6

We acknowledge the financial support of the Government of Canada through the
Book Publishing Industry Development Program (BPIDP) and that of the
Government of Ontario through the Ontario Media Development Corporation's
Ontario Book Initiative. We further acknowledge the support of the Canada
Council for the Arts and the Ontario Arts Council for our publishing program.

ONTARIO ARTS COUNCIL
CONSEIL DES ARTS DE L'ONTARIO

A portion of this novel appeared as a story in Secrets: Stories Selected by Marthe
Jocelyn, *Tundra Books, 2005.*

Design: Sean Tai
Typeset in Garamond

Printed and bound in Canada

1 2 3 4 5 6   11 10 09 08 07 06

For Frank and Shirley, and for Ann

ACKNOWLEDGMENTS

Thanks, as always, to Kathy Lowinger for her forbearance, and for her insightful comments and suggestions, and to Sue Tate for her patient and skillful copyediting. I also want to show my gratitude to my writing sisterhood for their advice, encouragement, comfort, and cheer, and, as always, to my family, close and extended, for their much-appreciated support.

Many years ago, when I first became interested in the woman known as Mother Barnes, the Witch of Plum Hollow, I was able to find information about her from her great-granddaughter, Lera Joynt of Smiths Falls, Ontario. I am grateful to her for helping me find research material, some of which I have altered to suit my story.

A Very Fine Line

1

They didn't tell us at school until Tuesday. At first everything went as usual. We clomped into the classroom while Miss Boyle wrote the date on the blackboard: December 8, 1941. She waited until we hung up our coats at the back and were sitting at our desks. "Class," she began, "something terrible has happened." She looked sharply at us, as if any of us could be at fault. "One of your classmates has disappeared from her home!"

Everyone got very quiet, twisting, craning to see who wasn't there. I turned around. No Faye Wirt sitting behind me. She hadn't been there on Monday, either, but everyone had thought she was sick. Now all eyes were on her empty desk, as if it could reveal an important clue. You could hear a rising drone of questioning and amazement and speculation.

I sat quietly, looking down at my own desk because I didn't care. No, that's not true. I was glad: no more pencil shavings poured down the back of my blouse, no more eraser bits blown into my hair. Faye Wirt had been mean to me from the day I arrived in grade eight, after skipping grade seven. No more painful jabs from the end of her ruler. Let her stay lost forever.

The *Kempton Mills Banner* lay open on the kitchen table when my sisters and I got home that afternoon. "Did you hear about this?" Adele, my mother, asked me. "Isn't she in your class?"

My sisters crowded around to read. Most of the front page was about Japan attacking Pearl Harbor and about the Americans and about the war in Europe. Right at the bottom was the heading GIRL FOURTEEN MISSING SINCE SATURDAY. It seems that Faye Wirt's father told the police that he had been out late Saturday night. When he got home, there was no sign of Faye. He thought she might have spent the night at a friend's house, but when she didn't come home on Sunday, he reported her missing. *Anyone knowing her whereabouts is asked to contact the police.*

Adele humphed. It was no secret what she thought of "those Wirts." The father, a staggering drunk, and the mother, well, she'd felt sorry for the mother – a timid mouse of a woman who'd worked for Adele at one time. She died suddenly, about two years ago. Fell down the stairs. Adele thought there was more to it. "Wirt had a hand in it, I'm willing to bet," she'd said at the time. The youngest, Faye, had sisters and brothers who had left town long ago. One of the girls ran off with some man and two of the boys had served time in jail, or so the rumor went.

Adele said sourly, "I expect she'll have gone through the ice on the river. This is such a dangerous time of year." She shuddered as if she regretted her tone and shook her head. "For the child's sake, I hope not, poor thing, but it's the first thing you think of."

It wasn't the first thing I thought of.

The Provincial Police and police from nearby towns were called in to help with the search. They dragged the river bottom, but found nothing.

The following week, just before the bell rang, the teacher said that the police wanted to look at the contents of Faye's desk. They had already searched the Wirts' house for clues. "Rosalind," she said to me. "Look inside and bring everything up to the front."

I didn't really want to, but I peered in. Not much in it – old maps she'd colored, some tests she'd never taken home – 26 out of 50; 4 out of 10. She had already failed a grade. There were the usual schoolbooks and scribblers and two overdue library books. I held everything in one arm while I reached to the back for something metal, flat, small. It was a hair barrette painted blue, but some of the enamel had chipped off. The curious thing was that just holding it in my hand made me feel off balance and hot. I let it fall to the floor. At the same time, I managed to drop all the other stuff.

"Good heavens, Rosalind!" the teacher said. "Pick it all up. Do you need help?"

I shook my head. My face was red, of course, but I picked the stuff up and plunked it on the teacher's desk, all except the barrette. The bell went and everyone grabbed their coats and lined up at the door. I bent over to pick up the barrette and immediately my head began to ache. I stared at it, at the pattern of chipped enamel. Quickly, I put it into the pocket of my dress, too rattled to even wonder whether it was a clue. I hurried then to take my coat and follow the others outside. My head was pounding like feet running.

I don't know why, but I had this strange sick-to-my-stomach yet excited feeling that I had been told something, a secret. A secret I must keep to myself. I hate secrets. To get it out of my head, I counted the houses on both sides all the way up Hill Street. *Twenty-nine, thirty, thirty-one.* It was working. *Thirty-two. . . .*

"I'm worried about Rosalind." My mother was talking to Aunt Lydia. It was close to Christmas, not quite two weeks after Faye Wirt's disappearance. "She's becoming very . . . peculiar. I sometimes wonder if she isn't a little touched in the head." Lydia made some sort of sound of denial or surprise. I knew what was coming.

Only the day before, Adele had said that Faye must surely have met her death in this cold weather, otherwise someone would have caught sight of her. That's when I told her that she wasn't dead. The barrette I'd rescued from her desk was now in the woods behind our back garden. I'd shoved it into a hole in a tree.

"How do you know?" Adele had asked me.

She looked at me so intently that I blushed because I had this strong feeling that I wasn't supposed to tell. I shrugged. "Everybody at school says she probably hopped a train." Adele had raised her eyebrows, as if she hadn't believed me.

Sometimes I get little memory flashes of Faye pressed up tight against the back wall of the school, as if hiding from someone. Or running. I've seen her running through people's back gardens.

The biggest reason I didn't like Faye Wirt was because she used to torment me by making up lies about me. She said my family was full of lunatics and freaks and witches. "No, yours is," I said back. She just laughed at me in this really sarcastic way she has. So I said, "Yours is full of robbers and murderers and drunk men." This I knew to be true, or nearly true, even though her insult to me had been made up. She got all red in the face and stared hard at me, as if she wanted to hurt me and make me cry. It's impossible to like someone like that. Besides, we had some very famous people in our family. One of my ancestors, Adam Kemp, settled this town and named it.

"But," Aunt Lydia was saying, "Rosalind's always been such a clever little piece."

"Oh, she's clever enough. It's just that she's taken to – how should I put it – knowing things, although she denies it."

My mother and my aunt didn't know I was sitting on the floor behind the sofa, peeling off little pieces of wallpaper, which I did partly because I was lonely, and partly because I wanted us to get new wallpaper.

"Oh, dear," Lydia said. She drew in a breath. "Let's hope not. I'm sure it's nothing. She's just at that difficult age. I wouldn't worry."

Adele said, "She's not like the others, nothing like."

"Well, watch and wait," Aunt Lydia said, getting up to leave. "That's all you can do for now." There was a pause while she looked for her gloves. "As you know, Adele, there's sometimes a very fine line between the real world and, well, shall we just say, the world of make-believe."

"Oh, I know that," my mother sniffed, but not because she was crying or anything. "It's just that I never know what's going through her head. Do you remember me telling you about the Wirt girl who disappeared?"

"She's still missing, I hear."

"I think Rosalind knows something, or maybe she's bothered by something that she's not telling us." I stopped picking at the wallpaper. "She doesn't confide in me the way her sisters do. It used to be that girls were an open book. I'm sure we were."

"Of course we were."

I tried to stop listening because I didn't want to think about Faye Wirt. I didn't want to remember how she always hung around the school as if she had no home to go to. In her great big shoes. Nothing ever seemed to fit her.

"When I think about it," my mother said, "she's been a trial from the day she was born."

I tried to remember what horrible pranks I might have got up to as a newborn baby, but that was going back a little too far, even for me.

*

Normal people don't really remember their babyhoods. I do. Bits of it. Come to think of it, though, no one has ever accused me of being normal. My christening I remember, and the great gray vaulted ceiling of the church, high as the sky with wisps of pastel clouds streaming past. Pinks, watery-green, satiny-blue. No one believes me, but it's true. Well, maybe not the clouds. But, I remember God swooping down on me in a big white dress, dripping water on my head and down my neck, and I hollered blue murder (Vanessa says that was the minister). I remember him pronouncing my name – Rosalind Rose Kemp – all rolling and hollow, as if he had taken a bite out of a hot potato. My father whispered, "It's all right now, it's all right," and my mother gently mopped my neck with a soft hanky. That's when I believed I was inseparable from my mother.

Afterwards, at home, I remember the old aunts, parts of them at least, Mother and Aunt Lydia's maiden aunts.

Smells stay in a person's memory. I remember the date squares being passed around. They smelled like spicy winds from desert lands. (I just made that up now, actually.) I remember I tried to grab one off the plate, but someone swished it away and shouted, "No-no!" My father gave me a plain sugar cookie that had no smell at all, but it exploded in my baby hands and went all over the place, and I wasn't allowed to eat it off the floor. "No-no," they all said. "Dirty-dirty."

And I remember the sharp smell of tea and lemons, and stumbling against a succession of knees as I toddled from chair to chair to couch. I was so cute, they all said. I was the star of the show. A whole collection of relatives was there, but, unlike the maiden aunts, they remain scribbley, as if they'd been colored by a baby, outside the lines.

I was christened rather late in my babyhood. I guess they'd forgotten about me, as often happens to the youngest in a large family. My cousin Cornelius Merrick was christened at the age of three months. An only child. He remembers nothing.

Vanessa always tells me that I was too young to remember any part of it. "You would only remember what you've been told," Vanessa insists, "for instance, the way we laughed forever-after about the faces Marietta made."

Maybe she's right. But, I think she's wrong.

I remember how they smelled. I don't think anyone wanted to sit near the old aunts because they reeked. I remember two bony knees and, beneath them, shanks, hard as the legs of the kitchen table. I know because I crawled under Great-Aunt Nell's long skirt until someone hauled me out. Nearby was another set of stale knees, Great-Aunt Eileen's, pudgier, with hands resting on them, fingers beckoning me. Above my head floated voices: "You'll have to tell her when she's old enough, Adele," they said to my mother, "and if you won't, we will." I was pretty sure that was what they said. Or maybe I'm just making that up, too.

"I won't have superstitious stories and bold-faced lies put into her head," my mother said.

"It's not lies," one of the old aunts said. "Would your own grandmother live a lie? Look at this child. Just look at the eyes on her." A hand tilted back my almost-bald little head. Other hands grabbed me by the armpits, held me aloft, eyeball to eyeball, until the shriek I'd been nurturing burst upon their eardrums and I was snatched from further examination by my mother.

I have very dark eyes, so brown, they're almost black. Actually, they *are* black.

My sister Marietta, meanwhile, continued to annoy the old birds by pulling the corners of her mouth up and the corners of her eyes down and sticking out her tongue.

"And as for this one," growled one of the old dames, grabbing Marietta by the front of her dress and giving her a good shake, "she'll be the death of herself, so she will." She raised her voice to make sure Marietta got the full impact of her prediction. "You'll spit in the face of fate once too often, my girl!"

Mother scooped me up with one arm and shooed Marietta ahead of her, away from the aunts. Beatrice, my oldest sister, collected Vanessa and the twins and sat all three of them on the settee. She told them she'd wring their necks if they so much as let out a peep. I could see them over my mother's shoulder. When Bea turned her back, Vanessa said, "Peep."

Father sat making polite conversation with the guests, and Aunt Lydia followed us into the kitchen whispering, "They're old, Del. They just say whatever comes into their heads. Don't pay any attention."

"I never dreamt they'd come," Adele hissed, "at least, not both of them." She gave Lydia a pointed look that my baby brain couldn't understand, as though they shared a secret. And then she pursed her lips, tight enough to suck spit through a straw. "Every time they look at me," Adele said, "I see scorn in their eyes. They think I'm dreadful."

Lydia put a finger to her lips and nodded toward Marietta. "Little pitchers," she said.

Adele let out a deep breath. She tried to put me down, but I clung like a bat. She shook Marietta by the shoulder. "And what in the world possessed you, Miss Boldy-brat? Such a way for a girl your age to behave! I was shocked, just shocked."

Marietta merely raised her eyebrows and rolled her eyeballs up so high, you could see only the whites.

Adele dropped wearily onto a kitchen chair with me on her knee. "I don't mind going to visit *them,* but every time those old biddies come here, something happens. They spoil everything."

Aunt Lydia stroked her head. "There-there," she said. "What is, is. You know they're good-hearted, in their own way."

Everyone left as shadows slanted deeply into what remained of the afternoon. Propped against my mother's hip, I saw everyone wave at the departing guests – Mother, my sisters clustered around her skirt, and even Marietta, standing a little apart. She'd been sent to her room, but Father had let her come down after five minutes. The great-aunts lumbered out to a waiting automobile, high and square, some early Ford model it might have been. They were heaving and shifting to fit themselves around a third person occupying the backseat. The driver must have been a neighbor, or someone hired for the day, as they didn't own a car themselves. He wedged himself in behind the steering wheel, slammed the door, and, an instant before they rumbled from sight amidst a spiral of dust, someone, or something, pig-faced, pressing against the small rear window, leered at us with squint-eyed loathing. Mother stared wildly, as if she would run after them. Father turned her away and hurried her back to the house.

"They love to torture me," Adele said.

"They're flesh and blood, Adele, yours and mine, and they have every right to see one of their own relatives christened. You owe them that much," said Lydia.

"Harpies!" Adele said.

3

Our father died six years ago, when I was six. My memory of him is limited to only a few tiny scenes because he was always at work, or in his study at home. His last Christmas stands out, though. It's a good memory, even though it makes me out to be a bit of a nitwit.

My mother kept shooing me out of the kitchen, where she was rolling out piecrusts and muttering under her breath when they developed holes or stuck to the rolling pin. My sisters wouldn't let me into their rooms because they were wrapping presents. My father was in his study, staring into space or at graphs and numbers, as he always did when he was at home.

To amuse myself, I tried walking all around the sitting room without touching the floor, something I had learned from Vanessa. I did pretty well, going from chair to couch to lamp table without knocking over the lamp. I stepped onto the radiator and then managed to leap over to the piano bench, from which I climbed to the top of the upright piano.

From there I had to grab the plate rail, up near the ceiling, and dangle high above the floor, inching my hands along to get to the open door where I would be able to put my feet on the doorknobs and swing over to a chair. Unfortunately, I knocked a picture of my grandfather off the wall, and it fell with such a crash and shattering of glass that everyone came running, and there I was, hanging by my fingernails trying to swing my feet over to catch the doorknobs. And missing.

The rest was all shrieks and demands and calling on the Lord and confusion, and I landed on my back on the floor with the wind knocked out of me. Next thing I knew, once I could take a breath, I was on my father's knee on a chair in the drawing room, where we had the Christmas tree up and decorated.

My father was a man of few words. He simply sat with me, gazing at the lighted tree. I began to fidget and complain in the long silence, but he held firm. The next moment (perhaps he had a notion about taming wild creatures) he began to sing, shakily at first, quietly lest anyone hear. "Si-a-lent night, ho-a-ly night," he sang, his voice soft as falling snow, tender as a kiss, enchanting me into good behavior.

He died a few months later. One night, during a severe asthma attack, he stopped breathing.

On the day of his funeral, I went into his clothes closet and shut the door. Feeling around in the dark, I found his size eleven shoes and put my feet into them. I squatted on the backs of them, my face wet and streaked, and sang to myself, si-a-lent night, ho-a-ly night. The fragrance of his

tweed jackets and pipe smoke and shaving lotion and polished leather shoes meant he hadn't gone too far away.

"Rosalind!" I heard my sisters call. "You can't wear over-
alls to a funeral."

But I did. I fought so hard, they finally gave up on me
and my scruffy play clothes. I felt my mother's eyes, but she
didn't say anything about how I looked. I don't think it was
me she actually saw.

Before the funeral, before all the relatives and friends
began to arrive at Hill Street, my mother sat in his chair, tall
and collected, ankles crossed. Her face was pale, but her eyes,
pink from crying, were determined, staring straight ahead.
I wanted her to look at *me*. He was *my* father, after all. I
needed comfort. I climbed onto her lap, but she just sat still,
her arms on the armrest. "Get off, please, Rosalind. You're
too heavy."

Our father was buried near a tall obelisk, a monument in
the family plot in the cemetery, his name carved into the base
near the names of his forebears. My mother glowered at the
leafless trees, the collar of her black coat turned up against
the March wind. It became clear to me for the first time that
she had thoughts in her head that were not necessarily about
me, her youngest child. We were two separate people. That
was when I began to think of her, privately, simply as Adele.

The Kemp girls, people called my sisters and me, as if we
came as a boxed set. We were sprawled around the drawing

room like bodies washed up after a shipwreck. A fire in the grate made us drowsy. We'd just finished decorating the Christmas tree while, outside, a blizzard pelted the windows. Empty cardboard boxes from the glass ornaments and crumpled tissue paper lay scattered over the floor. Adele was putting dinner in the oven, but soon she would be harping at us to tidy up. Music wafted from the gramophone.

I was twelve-and-a-half years old that winter. The twins, fifteen and identically skinny, had nabbed the couch and lay at either end, stockinged feet beside each other's cheek. Lamps shed cones of light on the weekend funnies. They each had a page.

Our oldest sister, Beatrice, was the only one not here. She was a grown-up married lady now, and when she came home, always sat with her knees together and her head high. She was the family beauty, as everyone reminded us.

Beatrice had the knack of applying just a hint of color to her high cheekbones, and knew how to pin her hair back on one side to achieve an effect. I guess that's how she managed to lure Dalton Kirby away from Marietta. Marietta had had a crush on him for four years, and just when he'd begun to notice her, Beatrice swanked up, batted her eyelashes, and the next thing we all knew they were settling on a wedding date.

"I'd never do that to you," I said to Marietta at the time.

"Sure you would, Ros; we all would."

Marietta says she's over it, but I don't believe her.

Vanessa came spot in the middle of the family, if you counted the twins as a single unit, and most people did. She was home from secretarial school for the Christmas vacation. Her hair curled naturally every which way, too unruly to stay tucked behind her ears. It gave her a wild look, as if she'd just come in out of a hurricane. Beatrice once said, "Let your hair grow, for heaven's sake. It will draw attention away from your snubby little nose." Vanessa refused to talk to Bea for three days. Now she was reading the business section of the newspaper. The skirt of her dress was skewed up above her knees as she sprawled crosswise in what had been Father's easy chair. She didn't care. The music from the Victrola blared on.

Marietta was the second oldest. She sat on the floor, slouched over the front section of the paper – the curve of her back against the radiator, her legs splayed out in front like a rag doll. She was home for the weekend from the city hospital, where she was doing a year of interning. She had already graduated from university and was officially a doctor.

Doctor Marietta Kemp. It's pretty hard to imagine your own sister fixing people. If she'd been a brother, maybe, but in our family, we specialized in girls, six in all. The floor lamp above enveloped her in yellow warmth. People said she was big boned, which apparently explained a lot. And they said it was one thing to *be* intelligent, but it was a pity she had to *look* intelligent, too. She looked just fine to me. She was my hero.

Faintly we heard the clanging bell of the dependable six fifteen pulling into the railway station on the edge of town, announcing evening. Marietta glanced at her watch. So did Vanessa. All over Kempton Mills, people would check the time and wind their watches, a town habit.

The train station in Kempton Mills was a bustling place. If we were there to meet someone, or to see someone off, I loved to run beside the train as it left town, gathering speed. I always felt a resonance vibrating in the marrow of my bones as I kept pace with the big engine, *chuff-chuff-chuff*ing as it got up steam. The howl of its whistle would fill my ears, my head, push aside all thoughts not connected with trains. I would stop then at the end of the platform, pulling up my socks that always slipped down into my shoes when I ran. I listened to the melancholy call rising, falling, fading as the train picked up speed, heading farther and farther away. It made me shiver.

This evening, with Christmas only a few days off, I lay on my stomach on the floor near Marietta, drawing pictures on the back of my last leftover roll of wallpaper. I had a book on it to keep it flat. Sometimes I put my head down on my arm because I was tired. I also had a bit of a headache.

As I finished portions of my drawing, I allowed it to roll back on itself. I guess I wanted the roll to be endless, but, of course, it wasn't. I hoped my mother would start looking critically at the drawing room walls, especially behind the couch, and call in the paper-hanger before my roll was finished. One section showed the life cycle of my family with me at the center. Another section, the one I was working on, was a whole cast of characters, in fact, everyone I knew, except Faye Wirt.

Our mother came into the drawing room to lift the needle at the end of the recording. "Now, wasn't that stirring?"

There was a chorus of *mmm*'s that lacked depth of feeling.

"Just imagine what an entire opera would be like onstage!"

"*Mm-hmm.*"

Her goal in life, it seemed, was to have us all turn out to be a credit to her. All we had to do was be able to recognize classical music, behave in a ladylike manner, make ourselves attractive, speak in cultured tones, and accompany her to church every Sunday so that she could show us off and hear people say, "My dear, they are such a credit to you." We represented her life's work.

"I hope you're going to put away all these boxes."

"*Mm-hmm.*"

Adele wound up the Victrola and put on Beethoven. "Make sure you listen to this, you younger girls," she said. "It will be an inspiration for you to practice your piano pieces."

Für Elise raced through the sound box. Adele had wound the crank too far. She paused at the door. "Look at the two of you, sprawling all over the floor. Marietta, you should know better. Rosalind, if you must draw pictures, sit properly at a table. You'll ruin your eyes being so close to your work."

"I like being close to my work. I can see it better."

Vanessa said, "I don't know why you don't take that child to have her eyes examined, Mother."

"Perhaps I should," Adele agreed.

"And her head, at the same time," Vanessa added, training a newspaper telescope on me.

Sylvia and Cynthia traded sections of the funnies.

Her remarks didn't bother me; I was used to them. Adele glanced with mild reproach at Vanessa before turning her attention once more to me. The phone rang then, and with a frown, Adele went hurriedly to answer it. A ringing phone always meant bad news as far as Adele was concerned, until she answered it and discovered that it was only someone who merely wanted to interrupt her day. For some reason, as it rang, I thought it sounded like a baby crying, which was just plain stupid. A boy baby.

We could hear Adele in the hall, chirping into the phone, "Oh, my dear, how wonderful. How exciting! How are you feeling?"

"Bea," I said quietly.

Before long, Adele returned beaming. "You'll never guess what. Beatrice is going to have a baby." There was much excited chitchat about all of us becoming aunties. "And I'll be a grandmother," Adele said. "Oh, dear, how old that makes me feel!"

"About time we had some boys in this family," I said cheerfully.

"What are you talking about?" Adele asked. The twins propped themselves up on one elbow to stare at me. "How do you know it's a boy?" Cynthia asked. The others looked puzzled. Adele had a peculiar look on her face.

In her next breath, Adele said, "Rosalind, you're quite

pale. Are you feeling all right? You know, it's not healthy to spend so much time indoors doodling pictures. You should have been outside all afternoon, sliding down hills with your friends."

I looked out the window at the blowing snow. "What friends?"

"Exactly! If you'd been outside playing, you'd have a dozen friends."

"These are my friends," I said, unrolling part of my mural to reveal a long queue of characters in various human poses.

I used to have friends, but not lately. Kids think I'm always staring at them. They say I give them the heebie-jeebies. I'm not really staring, just looking.

Adele bent over the scroll, studying it from different angles, frowning. "What is it supposed to mean?" she asked.

"Nothing," I said.

"But, look at how you've drawn these people! If they *are* people. Are they cartoons?"

"No."

"But that's not the way people look." Adele straightened up.

"That's the way they look to me."

"I think you can draw nicer pictures than that, Rosalind! All eyes, that one is. And a mouth that takes up this one's whole face."

Marietta studied the drawings, too, and the others glanced over to find out what the fuss was about. It was well known that Marietta had the brains in the family. It was a fact suspected when she finished high school at sixteen, and proven when the university accepted her into the faculty of medicine. Looking up from my drawings, she said, "Ros is artistic. I think we have to remember that. She sees things differently from the rest of us. I think if we don't recognize this, we're going to give the kid a complex." This was said with the authority of a student of science.

"A complex! My word! Marietta, I do think," Adele said, "that if your scientific education were a little more confined to aches and pains and pills, it would be a great deal more useful."

The recording of *Für Elise* scampered to the end and scraped pleadingly to be released. Adele's attention fell on me, again. "You're just going through a phase, Rosalind. We all have our little phases." She came over and put her hand on my forehead, shaking her head at my pictures.

I will admit that I felt Adele was being overly critical of my drawings. They didn't look bizarre while I was drawing them. But once they became a topic of conversation, I could see how ugly they were. They weren't childlike scrawls – I was twelve, after all – they were just, well, grotesque.

I hate going to bed, usually, but I went up early that night. Marietta came into my room to see if I was all right. I was scrunched down under the covers because I was freezing for some reason, but I sat up when she came in. "Do you ever get the feeling," I asked, "that something is going to happen, and then it does?"

"Sometimes, I guess. It's called women's intuition."

"Oooh," I said, "so that's what it is."

"So you think Bea's baby will be a boy, do you?"

"Maybe I just have girls' intuition."

I snuggled back down under the covers. If I kept quiet, this feeling I had would probably go away. It gave me a bad taste in my mouth. I felt that a change was coming, that my life was about to take a new direction. It was as if I had somehow got aboard a special train without a ticket, destination unknown.

4

The snow stayed around right through the holidays. My cousin Cornelius begged to have me come for a visit after Christmas until New Year's. Aunt Lydia said yes, of course, because she rarely says no to her son.

Mother helped me pack. "I should be going with you, or the twins."

"No need."

"You'll be all over the countryside with Corny."

"We're big enough."

"I don't want you visiting the old aunts."

I looked up from folding my flannel nightgown. "How come?" I knew she meant Great-Aunt Eileen and Great-Aunt Nell. I'd never visited them before and wondered what made her think I would now.

She frowned, placing a sweater in the bottom of my small suitcase. "It's not a fit place. Don't ask why. You're not to go and that's all there is to it." I began scrabbling under the bed for my slippers. "Do you hear me?"

I plunged my slippers on top of my nightie on top of the sweater and nodded.

"Get your toothbrush. And put in those long-legged snuggies, you'll need them out there. Lydia's house is drafty." She sighed. "This all goes against my better judgment."

"I'll be good."

"Your concept of good falls considerably short of mine," she said. "Well, Lydia will use her head, I trust, and keep you under her thumb."

After the great flu epidemic, Lydia and my mother were the only ones left in a family once boasting seven girls. They tended to live in each other's pockets a little, even though about forty miles separated them. My mother was the youngest in the family and Aunt Lydia liked to tell her what to do. In the radio play of our lives, Lydia was the director.

I felt grown up, traveling alone by train. I breathed against the frosted window to melt a peephole. Scraping at the crystals with my fingernails, I could make out blue-white fields speeding past, waves of snow rolling along, and fences here and there damming them back. A shadow of steam from the engine waved like a Sunday-school banner.

Corny would be glad to see me, all bustle and wagging. Aunt Lydia would be as crisp as burnt toast, and Uncle John, pipe in his mouth, would be all woolly and smoky, like snow pants drying on the wood box next to the stove in the kitchen.

At the little country station near the village of Plum Hollow, I jumped down quickly from the coach, my suitcase bumping against my leg. I didn't want the conductor to think I needed help. The engine *whooshed* and I was in a cloud of steam, hidden in a half-world. I could make out Uncle John waving, but Corny was barely visible. And then I saw his face splitting into a grin, the kind of grin you see painted on a clown's face, his head turned so that only his good side was visible. Behind me, the train wheezed and chuffed and tooted good-bye.

Except for his earflapped hat and bulky coat, he looked the same as he had last summer. Squashed together in Uncle John's car, we punched each other on the leg a couple of times, until I said, "Quit it." We drove slowly along the concession road, cushioned on either side by bolsters of plowed snow. We turned in at the Merricks' lane, where the farmhouse rose tall and narrow against the cold sky. It looked held in, like a proud corseted lady, an Aunt Lydia kind of house.

No sooner were we through the kitchen door with our coats off than Aunt Lydia made us stand back-to-back, to make sure Corny was still taller. He was. "Scrawny, the both of you," Uncle John said. We were within a few weeks of being the same age. Aunt Lydia had had to wait eight long years for her little Cornelius. When you're the youngest in the family, if you sit quietly long enough, you pick up information like that. I once heard my mother tell a friend, "For the first five months, Lydia didn't even know that she was expecting."

"Oh, surely she would suspect."

"She thought she had a tumor."

"Oh, my Lord."

She finally went into town to consult a doctor and that's when she found out about Corny. When he was born, he became her little miracle, birthmark and all.

Corny has what is called a port-wine stain on his face. It's a huge purplish red birthmark that covers nearly the whole of one side of his face. It looks grotesque until you get used to it. Aunt Lydia says it's a sign from heaven that he's destined for great things – perhaps prime minister of Canada. Corny thinks he's destined to haunt houses. He doesn't worry about it much, though. He never looks in the mirror, if he can help it. "If I can't see it, it's not there," he says. When people stare at him, he stares back and crosses his eyes.

Aunt Lydia had high hopes for her boy. Goals, she said. I saw her sizing me up and tightening her lips. "You're beginning to develop a waist," she said suspiciously, as if I'd done it on purpose, as if it would spoil her plans for Corny. "You'll soon be a grown-up young woman."

I made a sour face and Corny laughed. I never wanted to be all prissy and polite and bulgy like my mother, or like her friends. Or even tall and sucked in like Aunt Lydia. I was happy the way I was – wiry, strong, nimble, ready for anything.

Corny grabbed my suitcase, loping down the hall with it. "Come see my invention," he shrieked, over his shoulder. He didn't have a normal tone of voice. When he was happy, he tore people's ears apart. When he was glum, he mumbled. There was no in-between with Cousin Corny. He galloped ahead of me up the stairs, his head on a tilt.

He heaved my suitcase onto the bed in the spare room and dragged me by the arm into his. At one end of his room, on a table, lurked a contraption made of weights and pulleys and a maze of tunnels that came out at a broken piece of sharp metal fastened with wire to the end of a stick. "My new death trap," he explained.

He liked making death traps. All unsuspecting, his imaginary enemies – gangsters mostly, thugs, school bullies – would fall into one of his traps, and *chop!* Off with their heads, or arms or legs. Once he constructed a trap that allowed them to drown in melted candle wax. Sometimes they were pulverized by a slyly placed stone.

"Does it work?"

"Of course it works. Feel that blade. Sharp as a razor."

I ran my finger under the broken blade and promptly cut myself. It *was* a razor. I glared at Corny. He grabbed my hand and put my finger in his mouth, but I yelled and pulled away.

He made a face at the metallic taste of my blood. "That's how you stop bleeding," he said.

"No, it isn't." Allowing my finger to crook in front of me, I riveted my attention on it, imagining my blood vessels closing like gates. I concentrated so hard on my cut that I felt a tingling in my fingers, and in my toes, too, as if they'd gone to sleep. Within a few seconds, the blood stopped oozing.

Corny raised his eyes to meet mine. "How did you do that?"

"I don't know." He tried to grab my hand, but I pulled away to study his death trap with my hands behind my back. "This thing can't possibly work," I said.

He frowned, my cut forgotten in his need to defend his guillotine. "So, okay, it doesn't exactly work the way I planned."

It was close to working, though. It was just that, at the moment, a lot of volunteer effort on the part of the enemy was needed in order to have him achieve a state of decapitation.

"It's too quiet up there. What are you kids doing?" Aunt Lydia's voice reached us through the grating surrounding the stovepipe, which grew from the woodstove in the kitchen, up through the ceiling, and sprouted through the floor in Corny's bedroom.

"Nothing!" Corny shrieked.

"Well, come down and do nothing where I can keep an eye on you."

We exchanged baffled looks and thumped down the stairs. I always felt that I was on the brink of being in trouble in the presence of Aunt Lydia.

Near the end of my visit, the temperature took a sharp plunge during the night. We awoke to an ice-gray morning, with wind teasing the tops of the pines and then dropping to scud surface snow ahead of it across the fields. Corny and I slipped and staggered across the yard to take feed out to Aunt Lydia's hens, huddled together inside their personal feather-ticks. Our breath hung in front of us – wordless comic balloons.

In the afternoon, Uncle John went to Brockville on business and would be gone the rest of the day. Aunt Lydia had her sewing-circle ladies sitting with their work in the parlor. Corny and I were playing Chinese checkers at the kitchen table.

The doorbell rang. We raced to be first to answer it, but Aunt Lydia beat us to it. "Now who in the world . . . ?" she was saying. The village doctor stood in the open porch, bending away from the wind, clamping his hat to his head. His car idled in the laneway.

"Your aunt Nell's in bad shape, Lydia," the doctor said, stepping inside and removing his hat. "Took a weak turn in the night. They got a neighbor to call me. I went out to see her early this morning." He shook his head. "She's not good." He and Aunt Lydia exchanged a knowing glance. "I thought, when you go out, you could take her something for pain." He handed Lydia a brown bottle with a prescription label on it.

"Oh, dear, I've got the ladies here and John's away."

The doctor looked at Corny. "The young lad could take it, if he bundles up. I'd go again myself, but I've an office full of patients." Corny stepped forward, his chest rising. The doctor looked him squarely in the eye. "And don't do anything to rile poor Lucy. She knows something's up."

"He won't," Lydia called after him. "He's good with her." She closed the door.

"May I go, too?" I asked. I felt redness creep up the sides of my neck, remembering my mother's orders. I could hear the ladies in the parlor – someone talking, a little burst of laughter.

Aunt Lydia was preoccupied. "I'll make up a basket," she said. "Christmas cake and some beef tea."

"May I?"

"I think not." She frowned, as if she, too, remembered something.

"But there's nothing else to do." I followed her into the kitchen, where she hurriedly lined a four-quart basket with a tea towel. Corny was putting his coat on. More laughter from the parlor.

"Please?" I made my dark eyes as sad and lonely as I could.

Lydia looked at me and sighed. "Oh, I guess so. You can wait outside while Cornelius takes the basket in. You're to come straight back, both of you. You're not to stay, son, with your great-aunt Nell so sick." She handed him the basket.

Excited, I thrust my arms into my coat and pulled my tam down over my ears. Something was going to happen. I didn't know how I knew this, girls' intuition maybe, but it gave me a rushing feeling in my chest.

"Wait up!" I called to Corny, as the door slammed behind me. I wasn't about to do anything wrong. I was pretty sure my mother had only forbidden me to go into the house, and so I wouldn't.

"Let's take the shortcut," I said, when I caught up to him.

"How do you know about the shortcut?" The earflaps on his hat were tied under his chin, giving him a half-strangled look. The one on the left side of his face covered some of his birthmark, but what you could see looked almost bloody because of the cold wind.

I shrugged. "Just a guess." I led the way up a snowy lane, into a grove of trees.

"You've never even visited them before," he said.

"I know. Here, I'll carry the basket for a while."

Soon there were tree trunks on all sides, their bare branches groaning in the wind. "I'd better lead the way," Corny said. "You'll get us lost."

I followed for a while, lugging the basket, impatient. "If we veer to the left, we'll get there faster," I said. I got ahead of him then, but he bolted in front of me. He wanted to be the leader. I pushed him aside and, without meaning to, knocked him face-first into a low-hanging bough. "Sorry," I said.

"Now look what you did!" Blood ran from his nose over his upper lip.

"Put snow on it." I felt bad. We couldn't go very fast now with Corny scooping up snow every few minutes, only to throw it down when it got too cold on his nose. Behind us gleamed a red-spotted trail of frozen clots.

We were protected from the wind by the dense bush, but the cold bit through my mitts. Corny's nose stopped bleeding. At last we reached a clearing and saw, ahead of us, the shore of a frozen lake. On the far side huddled a stone house, smoke painted in the air above its chimney. "That's it, isn't it?" I said.

"Maybe." Corny looked sideways at me. "How come you know so much?"

I shrugged, surprised myself. "Just guessing. Maybe it's intuition."

"What's that?"

"It's like when you know something, but you don't know how you know it."

Corny snorted, as if he didn't believe me. I didn't mind all that much because, after all, he was a boy, and boys didn't have it. The ice, blue-black where the wind had swept it bare of snow, beckoned, and we bounded to the edge to test its strength. "You go first," Corny said.

At the very edge, the ice was lacy with cracks. I stepped out and the ice held. I dug with my heel and it held. I jumped on it. A resounding crack boomed throughout the entire lake, sending little shock waves of sound, causing a rumble in the lake's watery underbelly. We both screamed, but the ice held. "Go out a little farther," Corny said.

Oh, sure. "If I go through, you have to save me."

"I will."

I imagined the scene, my arms flailing in icy water, Corny running back and forth onshore, barking ideas: *Grab hold of something. Keep your head up.* It made me smile. I was testing myself against the ice's hidden power and feeling strong.

By the time I was halfway across, Corny joined me. We ran over hillocks of snow and slid on the windswept patches of ice, pausing to exclaim at a leaf, frozen in midswirl, and a frog, imbedded, limbs outstretched in immortal breast-stroke. The lake groaned in vain. We skipped ashore on the other side and heard its empty gulp.

"I hope we don't run into Lucy," Corny said.

"Who's Lucy?"

"I don't know. She lives with the old aunts, but we're not supposed to talk about her in public. She's batty."

"I'm not public," I said. "What does she look like?"

"The hind end of a pig."

"What's so batty about her?"

"She rocks back and forth like a rocking horse, and she keeps patting her mouth as if she can't remember what she was going to say."

"Is she old?"

"Don't know. Looks old, but I think she's young. Mother says she's smart and dumb at the same time. Born that way. The aunts take care of her because they never wanted her put away in an asylum, or any place like that."

We legged it over the snowbank bordering the road and trudged up the lane to the side of the house, keeping an eye out for Lucy. In spite of the cold, I felt sweat on my upper lip. "I'll wait right here for you," I said.

Corny took the basket and vanished into a dark shedlike entry. I waited, stamping my freezing feet.

Just then, a sound drew my attention to a wall of fire-wood stacked to the left of the entry. There was nothing there. I put my hands in my pockets and turned away. Again, the sound – whispery. A mouse, I decided.

"*Ssss,*" it said.

I wanted to believe it was a mouse, even a snake, cold as it was. But my thumping heart told me it was a human sound. "*Ssss.*"

My skin tingled, as if I were about to touch a hot burner. I whirled around. Behind me stood a slack-lipped, bug-eyed woman in a ragged fur coat. She clutched a stick of wood like a baseball bat aimed at my head. I stopped breathing. My legs turned to mush.

"Now, that'll do, Lucy!" A stump of an old woman appeared from the darkness of the doorway. "She won't hurt you, young lady. She likes to tease. Come in out of the cold, sure it's not a day to be out. Lucy, you get in here right this minute."

Lucy scuttled sideways into the house, shielding her backside from the old woman whose hand was raised in a threat. Helpless with fear, I allowed myself to be yanked in after her.

5

The large kitchen was warm and pungent with wood-smoke and spices. I took my eyes off the old woman long enough to notice a narrow staircase running up one wall of the room. Lucy was nowhere in sight. Corny sat at one end of a table, a plate in front of him, his mouth crammed full of gingery-smelling cake. The woman sat me down opposite him. His eyes met mine and he shrugged helplessly.

I watched the old hag bustle about the stove, creaking its door open, bending to look in. I wrapped my arms around myself, aware of how skinny I was beneath my coat. The old woman seemed to be sizing me up. I felt as if I'd stumbled into some old book of fairy tales.

"Need some meat on those bones, missy," the woman said. She shoved more wood into the stove. A big pot of water steamed on top. She busied herself over the basket we'd brought, taking out each item, squinting at it with one eye. "What's this? Medicine, is it?"

"The doctor sent it," Corny said.

She sat down on a chair near me and offered the plate of gingerbread. "No, thank you," I murmured, leaning as far as possible away from her. *I shouldn't have come. I should get up and leave.*

The old woman grinned, exposing a perfect row of teeth, lowers only. "Want some coffee?"

"Mmp!" My lips were pressed tight. I pushed my hair back under my tam. Except for the pounding of my heart, we sat in silence while Corny wedged more gingerbread cake into his face. I wanted to signal him that we should leave, but he wouldn't look at me. The woman reached for a pair of wire-rimmed spectacles on a shelf beside the stove and put them on. She inspected me.

"So. The young lad tells me you're my niece Adele's girl, the youngest. I'm your great-aunt Eileen. Your sisters are well?" The words sounded chewed. I nodded. "All still at home?"

"Three are away," I managed.

"Your mother had six sisters, too, and her the youngest. Did you know that?"

"I only have five," I said.

Eileen wheezed out a laugh. "We were there at your christening, Nell and me. Up and about then, Nell was. You were done late, a toddler. How old are you, now?"

"Twelve."

"Time you were told," she said. "May never come a better chance with Nell in the state she's in, and Lord only knows how long she'll last." She pocketed the bottle of medicine.

"Come along then, girl." With both hands on my shoulders, she pitched me out of the chair, forcing me to my feet. I tried to clutch Corny's arm, but he shrank away.

"Just go," he whispered. "They won't hurt you if you act polite."

Still grasping my shoulders, Eileen tried to escort me from the kitchen, but I balked, wriggling to get free.

"*Ssss!*" I heard then. Leaning over the banister, Lucy's pug-nosed face threatened from under her heavy brow. She started down the stairs, and that got me moving. Through the dimly lit passage we went and into a parlor that reeked of coal oil and mothballs. We skirted the heating stove, a rocking chair, and a skimpy settee stiff from disuse. Great-Aunt Nell's bedroom was behind the parlor.

We stood at the foot of a square bed, anchored at the corners by spooled posts. On the bedside table, an orange jaw of false uppers propped against a Bible grinned at me – the other half of Eileen's teeth, I guessed. In the bed lay a tissue-paper skeleton. I turned away.

"She won't bite you," Eileen said. "She doesn't look it, but she's awake. Nell!" she shouted, "Adele's child's here. The youngest."

The old woman opened one rheumy eye and then the other. I tried to back away, but felt Eileen's nudging fingers urging me closer.

"Are you the one, then?" Nell whispered. "Eileen, fetch me the spectacles." Eileen took them off her own face and wrapped them around her sister's wispy skull, curving them securely around her ears. Nell's eyes, immense now, focused on me.

"Lydia's sent you some kind of potion the doctor wants you to have." Eileen poured a dose into a small glass on the bedside table, raised her sister's head, and held the glass to her lips. Nell made a sour face, but swallowed it.

"You'll be wanting the teeth," Eileen shouted, setting the medicine glass down.

I watched in horror as the bedridden old woman reached out, clawed the bedside table, contacted the teeth, and with an immense effort, stretched her lips out of the way to allow her pale upper gums to receive the choppers. I tried to back out of range, but Eileen gripped me firmly.

Nell wheezed, "They told me once . . . better not to mention it. 'I don't want her told,' your mother said to me . . . oh, it was a while ago now." The old woman closed her eyes.

I allowed myself to breathe, hoping she'd drifted off to sleep. Or died.

She opened them suddenly. "Has it started, then?"

"Wh-what?"

"Do you see . . . patterns in things? Do you get a feeling for the future?"

My mother had been right – this was no fit place to be. "No!" I said sullenly. The smell of the old woman's breath made me queasy. Under the bed, I had noticed a chamber pot. Even with its lid on, I could smell that, too.

Eileen prodded me. "Speak nicely, girl, and speak up. Nell's hard of hearing."

"No, I don't!" I hollered.

The old woman's eyes bore into mine. "Little liar! I can see by your eyes it's been given to you. You've the gift, just as my mother had. You are your great-grandmother all over again."

I stood rooted, repulsed, enthralled. Too hot, I undid my coat, pulled at the neck of my sweater.

Eileen hissed in my ear, "For a long time, she's been wanting to tell you about our mother, your great-grandmother she was, so you listen. Practicing it for years, just for you."

Why me? My shoulders sagged. I listened as the old woman's voice wheezed out sentences that rolled over each other like a well-known song, or prayer.

"She was a comfort to all who knew her," Nell rasped. "Come from far and wide . . . Sir John A. himself, even . . . and kept herself and all us youngsters by telling people's fortunes . . . twenty-five cents a fortune, I believe it was. More for lost objects. And solved a murder, so she did . . . and went over to Brockville to watch the man hang."

The hook was baited; I was listening.

Sucking her teeth tightly into her gum, Nell said, "Irish she was, the seventh daughter of a seventh daughter. And a proud man was her father, an officer in the British Army." Perhaps it was the effect of the medicine, but Nell's voice flowed now, like a spill of satin ribbon.

"As the child grew, she was deemed prettier than all her sisters, with eyes that would catch you and hold you and read you like a book. And in all of Ireland, there was no match for the girl in beauty and wisdom. And her wisdom was uncanny and her mother feared for her, for she had the gift of foresight, which could bring her much pain. Nor would she be able to stop the pain, nor change fortune's path.

"And fair of hair she was with coal-black eyes, and she danced every dance at all the balls. And it happened, at last, that she danced her way into the heart of a lowly young sergeant in her father's company." The old woman moistened her lips with her tongue. "But her father forbade the marriage, whereupon she wept bitter tears. And so it came about that the two eloped to Canada, and my poor mother was cut off from the family who had loved and nurtured her through all her childhood years." Nell's voice fell silent.

"Is that the end?" I felt cheated. Surely there was more. Nell's breath came in long snores, as if she had fallen asleep. Timidly, I reached out and touched her shoulder. With a shuddering sigh, she again took up the tale.

"And at length my mother arrived on the shores of this very lake and made her home in a humble log house, not far from this stone one. And time passed, and soon it became known that my mother possessed powers beyond all understanding. And oh, they come from far and wide. When to plant the crops, they asked her, where to find lost items, and what would be the sex of their unborn child.

"And my father soon tired of the visitors and of his wife's gallivanting about the neighborhood, and although he forbade her to continue, he could not control her ways. No, sir, he could not. 'No sane man can live with a sage and a seer and keep his self-respect,' he said. He was not a man to be guided by a woman, and what man living would blame him if he left?

"And so leave her he did, and all of us children – me, Eileen, Rose, who was your grandmother, and two boys. Neither Eileen nor I ever married, but Rose, your grandmother, did and was blessed with the seven fine girls. In spite of his leaving, I still say Father was a good-hearted man, but sorely tried.

"And 'twas no time at all before word got round that our mother could read teacups with the skill of the Delphic Oracle, as she was sometimes called. And well I remember the buggies lined up while their owners waited their turn to have their fortunes told inside, at a small pine table. And many's the time I watched and listened, even as a grown woman, for I lived with my mother all her life.

"And I'd see how she'd swirl the teapot and give the leaves a good shake-up. And then must her fortune-seeker pour out a cup and carefully return the tea to the pot, making sure the leaves remained behind in the cup. 'Now turn it over,' she'd say, 'and twirl it.' And if all had been done correctly, at last she'd pick up the cup and read it.

"And once, I recall, she turned the cup back over. There was a party of young people come to have their fortunes told by the Wise Woman, as some called her. A bright sunny day in spring it was, and just the sort of entertainment the young people gloried in, for it lifted their spirits and gave them many a tale to tell at home.

"A young girl sat before her. I saw my mother's face cloud.

Her eyes, always bright as jet, grew dull. She didn't speak for an uncomfortable long time. At length, she handed the girl back her coin and said, 'I do not see a future in your cup.' And the girl looked down all sorrowful and embarrassed, as if she'd done a wrong thing, and my mother accompanied the girl to her waiting buggy and said to the driver, 'Take the long road home, lad.' But he laughed and wouldn't listen, and she stood in the road and watched the girl drive off with her friends." Great-Aunt Nell's lips smacked closed and then open as she tried to moisten them with her tongue.

I waited, unable to take my eyes off the old woman's face. Nell took a long breath. "And so it came about that my mother repeated to all those awaiting their turns, 'I can see no future.' And sadly she went back into the house, closing the door behind her, and admitted no one else for many days to come.

"And on their way back home, less than an hour later, the young girl whose cup showed no future was thrown from the buggy and killed in an instant, for the horses took fright from a passing train."

I felt a chill and shivered. Great-Aunt Nell stopped talking.

"And then what?"

Nell turned toward me, surprised. "Eh?"

"Wh-what happened next?"

Nell fixed her eyes on mine. "There was some called her witch. They used to burn witches. May still do, for all I know." Her labored breathing filled the room.

I broke the silence, my voice shrill with fear. "And was she?"

Nell wheezed. "And they'd call her in for the birthing of the babies. And for the laying out of the dead."

"Was she?" I said louder. I remembered Faye Wirt's taunt that our family was full of lunatics and freaks and witches.

The old woman's voice faded to a whisper. "And she was the seventh daughter of a seventh daughter."

She reached out a frail hand toward me. I shrank back until Eileen pushed me forward, pressed me to accept the old woman's hand. "She was not a witch," Eileen said. "She could always see her shadow. There's the proof against it. And if she couldn't, she'd light a candle. And many's the night you'd be coming along the path and look up and you'd see it, the shadow of her, through the window of the house."

I touched the trembling claw, dry as papier-mâché, its veins miniature purple mountain ranges, its tendons a fan of straight roads through them. "I put this story in your charge," she whispered, "because you're the one." Her dry fingers closed around my sweaty hand, as if we had a pact. "You've been given it." She closed her eyes.

"I'm not the one!" I said firmly. The two old women looked at me, both nodding, both smiling. "I'm not the one!" I screamed. I turned and ran, stumbling against furniture. Howling, I fled the house.

Lucy flew down the stairs, following me out the door. "Little sister! Little sister!" I heard, as I ran across the road and onto the ice. I stopped to button my coat and looked back. For the space of three heartbeats, we stared at each other.

"No!" I shrieked.

I followed the red petals of Corny's blood in the snow. I thought they grew bigger as I passed, splashes, pools. *Omens.* I was nearly home before Corny, with his questions, caught up.

"What happened?"

"Nothing. Just some made-up story she told me." When I turned to look at him, he was staring hard at me. I knew my eyes blazed, dark as jet.

I was glad it was nearly the end of my holiday. I went to bed early, without any dinner. Lydia thought I was sick, but I wasn't. The story old Nell had told me was stupid and silly. She was batty. They all were, especially Lucy. She hadn't called me little sister. I knew that, now. What she had said was, "Little miss, little miss." Once I'd settled that in my mind, I was able to curl up in bed and think of other things – snow, ice, darkness.

Corny came into my room a couple of times, but I closed my eyes and pretended to be asleep. "I know you're faking," he said.

I didn't care. I kept my eyes scrunched shut, hoping he'd go away. I didn't want to talk about the gibberish old Nell had told me. I couldn't remember it anyway. *Snow, ice, darkness,* I thought, and felt better.

"What was wrong with you last night?" Corny whispered next morning when I came down, starved, for breakfast.

"Nothing. I was just tired and chilled because it was so cold."

"Why did you run out of their house?"

"It was too hot, and I didn't like the smell."

I was afraid he was going to keep quizzing me, but just then Aunt Lydia turned off the kitchen tap and said, "What are you two whispering about?"

"Nothing," we said.

I spent a lot of time in my room after I got home. Every so often some part of Nell's story wormed its way into my head. "Stupid," I whispered. "As if anyone would believe it." In my own house, in my own room, where everything was familiar, clean, bright, normal, I was able to take deep breaths and tell myself none of it was true. Well, my great-grandmother's fortune-telling might be true. I'd heard that story before. But it had nothing to do with me. There must be lots of fortune-tellers around; whether or not they were any good is another matter. It's all just a game, anyway.

Great-Aunt Nell died shortly after my visit. Adele went to the funeral. When she came home, she looked terrible, as if she'd been through an ordeal.

CHAPTER

6

Each morning that winter, I trudged down the hill to school with the twins in their look-alike coats. Cynthia scurried to keep up, treading now and again on the heels of Sylvia's galoshes. *"Ouch,"* Sylvia said. "I walk on them too, you know."

"Sorry."

We didn't talk about anything much on the way to school. The twins didn't usually communicate with anyone but each other. They were in high school and had farther to walk.

I was in a grade eight class that included some pretty big kids – a couple of girls who should have been in high school but had failed somewhere along the way. Friends of Faye Wirt. I was the youngest and smallest girl in the room.

I didn't have any real friends at school. Skipping a grade had made me shy and a little wary of these bigger girls, who seemed always to be whispering about bosoms or boys, and they had a sharp odor about them that didn't seem to bother them. They treated me like an outsider, like someone who didn't yet know the password. I liked my flat skinny body just fine and hoped it would never change.

"Are you paying attention, Rosalind, or are you dreaming?" the teacher said.

"Yes, Miss Boyle," I answered, and everyone laughed. My face red, I opened the grade eight reader and stared at a poem we had to learn. As the class laughed, Miss Boyle, eyes atwinkle, tightened her lips into a little cat's mouth, making whiskers sprout darkly at its corners. Everyone called her Kitty behind her back.

At school after Christmas, I kept thinking about Faye Wirt for some reason. I remembered how her eyes had often looked puffy and red. One day Miss Boyle had slapped her ruler on Faye's desk to wake her up. She really *had* been asleep because she looked as if she'd been dreaming that someone was going to slap her desk, or maybe even hit her. She jumped awake and tried to hide her head in her arms. Everyone laughed.

Some kids thought she probably just ran away because she hated her drunken father. Some kids said her father had murdered her and buried her in the woods. One of Faye's friends, who wore bobby socks and high heels to school, said for sure she had hitchhiked to Hollywood. She'd seen her in a movie.

"Which one?" someone asked.

"I can't remember the name of it," she said, "but Faye was in it and she looked beautiful. She wasn't the star exactly, but it was a pretty good part for someone like her."

*

The only thing anybody at home talked about anymore was the war. Adele bemoaned the rationing of sugar and of gasoline. Although she seldom drove the car, she felt the rationing was a great imposition. When Beatrice had her baby, Adele wanted to be able to go and help her out as often as possible. And to arrive empty-handed, without so much as a cake, pie, or plate of brownies to celebrate the event, would be unforgivable.

When Marietta came home for a weekend, she was incensed about the conscription riots in Montreal. "What does the prime minister mean by 'conscription if necessary, but not necessarily conscription'?" She flung out an arm, as if she would shake the meaning out of the prime minister himself, and knocked over a glass of water. "Damn!" she said.

"Don't flail about, Marietta! And mind your language!" Adele mopped up the spill with her napkin to prevent an overflow onto the floor. "Having a scientific education does not excuse unladylike behavior."

Marietta still seemed unable to live up to the type of woman that fit in with Adele's ideals. "Why that child would want to take up the study of medicine is beyond me," Adele had said to Lydia one Saturday, her sister's day in town. They had had their heads together over a cup of tea while I quietly drew my silly pictures and listened in.

"It's entirely unbecoming in a young lady, not to mention unwholesome and morbid," she continued.

"Adele, the world is changing," Lydia replied.

"Yes, and not for the better. It's the biggest waste of an education I've ever heard of. Who would voluntarily choose to go to a lady doctor? Tell me that." There was silence. I guess Lydia hadn't been able to think of anyone.

One late February afternoon, Adele's bridge club met at our house. They were just winding down when I got home from school with a wicked headache. I craved sweets and so I hoped the ladies hadn't finished up the cakes and cookies they always had at these parties. Some of them had contributed to the sweets tray to avoid using up Adele's rations.

"Would anyone like more tea?" Adele asked. She sounded weary.

"Lovely," Mrs. Wilson said, easing herself away from one of the two bridge tables set up in the drawing room. She followed Adele across the hall to the dining room. Adele peeped into the teapot, polished to a luster that morning, and added a splash of hot water.

"I think we've spent more time chitchatting about the war than playing bridge," Mrs. Wilson said. She handed Adele her cup and saucer. Mrs. Musgrove stood beside her, sipping the last of her tea.

I pressed my fingers into my forehead, but stopped before Adele caught sight of me. She didn't approve of headaches. "People who complain of every ache and pain show a distinct want of moral fiber," she often said.

The ladies had gathered the cards, tallied the scores, and drifted into the dining room. Amidst the chatter of high points and low points and the clatter of teacups, I edged my way toward the sideboard and the last piece of cake.

"I wonder if I should have been in no-trump that last hand," Mrs. Musgrove said to no one in particular. She put her cup and saucer on the sideboard just as I was reaching for the lone piece of cake. My sleeve caught her cup, overturning it. The few remaining drops of tea spilled harmlessly into the saucer. She righted her cup, smiling at the spread of tea leaves, and raised her eyebrows playfully.

"Oh, now she's in for it," Mrs. Musgrove trilled. "You know what they say: she who spills the tea reads the leaves."

Embarrassed, I backed toward the pantry door hoping to escape, but Mrs. Musgrove merrily thrust the cup under my nose, cornering me. I bent over it and frowned.

"Well, gypsy, what's my fortune to be?"

All the ladies were beaming at me, joining the game.

"Isn't she petite?" someone said. "A regular pixie."

My cheeks reddened as I looked again into the cup. Rings of tea leaves were stacked near the bottom and others dotted one side, as if falling through space. Before I even thought about it, I mumbled, "You're going to get a lot of money, I guess."

The bridge ladies' tinkle of laughter rippled over my head. "That's the spirit, my dear."

"Isn't she a marvelous little thing?" one lady said.

"No cause for worry over the child, Adele. None whatsoever," said another.

I nabbed the well-earned piece of cake and made my getaway through the kitchen and up the back stairs.

By nine o'clock that evening, the entire bridge club knew about the death, following a heart attack, of Mrs. Musgrove's bachelor brother – the one who'd made a million in African diamonds. Mrs. Musgrove would inherit it all. I hid in my room all evening. Adele was called to the phone no fewer than seven times. "A mere child!" I heard her say. I tried to drown out the sound of my mother's voice by reciting the countries and capitals of South America. "A complete coincidence, of course!"

The telephone finally stopped ringing. I waited, scarcely breathing, for Adele to come tapping on my door. When she came in, her face was clenched in a series of horizontal lines – eyebrows, eyes, mouth. She sat on the end of my bed, where I was studying for a geography test. I put a finger on Venezuela and closed my eyes. The troubling image of Adele's face gave way to the location of Caracas.

"I think it's time we had a talk," she said, trying to look less severe.

"What about?"

Adele's face was pale, the skin under her eyes pouched. She looked old. She massaged the joints of her fingers, as if they hurt. "I don't like this game you're playing, Rosalind, pretending to make predictions about the future. It's silly."

I bit the edges off my thumbnail. "I didn't mean to." Adele reached out and took my hand away from my mouth. "They kept nattering at me to read the tea leaves. I didn't know Mrs. Musgrove's brother would die!"

"I'm aware of that. I'm not blaming you." Adele's eyes bore into mine. "But if you let yourself get into the habit of pretending these things are true, Rosalind, you might not be able to stop. People might think that you are, well, a little weak in the head. They would steer clear of you. I don't want you to get a reputation for being strange. I say this to you now, but I mean you to remember it forever."

I looked down at my geography text, wanting something else to think about, but I couldn't focus. "I could have made up something, I guess."

Adele frowned down at her hands, her finger joints red and a little swollen. "What did you see in the teacup?"

"Coins. A lot of them."

"Didn't you see tea leaves?"

I stared. "Well, yes. But they made a pattern, like stacks of coins. And then I couldn't see anything but the pattern."

"How did you know what the pattern meant?"

"I don't know," I said, surprised. "I think I just said the first thing that came into my head. I had to escape from Mrs. Musgrove's stupid teacup."

"I have two pieces of advice, Rosalind," Adele said. "Think before you speak. Also, don't tell everything you think you know." There was something guarded in her face as she said this, something secret. "And don't try to look so deeply into things that they become distorted. That way you won't see as much. The safest course is to skim the surface. Lift up thine eyes unto the hills."

She stood up, pulling in her stomach, straightening her spine. "I have a suspicion you've already heard the tales about your great-grandmother." She waited.

"Yes." My voice was small.

"I knew it! Lydia should have informed me. It's all foolishness, of course. My aunts, in their silliness, amusing themselves and anyone else who might listen with tales of my grandmother's supposed Delphic power!" I watched as Adele's eyes roamed the walls, the corners of the room. At length she turned a cold eye to me. "It's all a pack of lies. There's not an ounce of truth in it and there's to be no more tampering with it." With an effort, Adele made her features softer, said good night, kissed me briefly on the forehead, and paused, a new thought occurring. "And was there someone else in the house?"

"No," I lied.

"*Hmm.*" Adele let out her breath and narrowed her eyes, not knowing quite what to make of that. She said good night again and walked heavily out of the room.

7

Most of the snow had gone by the first week of March, and each day the sun was a little stronger and a little warmer. I barely noticed. School was becoming a torture; my marks were poor, not much better than Fay Wirt's used to be. I think my mind was filled to the brim with that ridiculous story Great-Aunt Nell had told me. In the daytime I worried about the lies she had tried to make me believe, and all night I was haunted by Lucy-dreams – nightmares, really. Yet, I wanted to go back to the stone house. Just once. Something needed to be set straight. I would have to wait for the Easter holidays, probably, more than a month away.

As it turned out, Aunt Lydia phoned one evening to see if I would like to go with them that very weekend to visit Uncle John's ailing sister, who lived in Watertown, New York. At first my mother said no. She was still cross with Aunt Lydia for allowing me to talk to the old aunts.

"It will be a cultural experience." Lydia tended to shout on the phone because of the party line. "Travel broadens the mind," she bellowed.

"She should stay home and study," Adele said.

"Cornelius won't go unless she comes along to keep him company. Could I leave him with you, if you won't let Rosalind come?"

Adele always found Corny a little too boisterous to suit her dignified ways, a little too shrill. "Well," she said, "I suppose Rosalind *could* go. But she'll have to take her books."

"Oh, yes, indeed," I heard Lydia say. "And so must Cornelius." She said that Uncle John had to go into town anyway and would pick me up after school on Friday. They would have me back by Sunday. Farmers, it seemed, had access to more gas than others.

Saturday morning we were up early, packed, and excited about going across the border into the United States. I had no thoughts to spare for the gray women in their gray house. Neither Corny nor I had ever been to another country and we wondered how much different it would look from Canada. Corny got into the backseat and I stood waiting for him to make room for me. "Shove over," I said.

"I'm sitting here," he said. "You'll have to go round." I went around the car with a disgruntled sigh and got in the other side. Even though I'd seen his face a million times, he needed to keep the raw-looking side away from me, thinking, I guess, that I could be fooled into believing his whole face was normal.

Corny and I had dutifully put our schoolbooks beside us

on the backseat, but we also had a stack of games to play. The baggage was in, Aunt Lydia had packed us a picnic, and off we went. Before we were halfway down the long lane out to the road, though, the engine died.

We waited patiently while Uncle John raised the hood of the car and tinkered with the engine. We waited, not quite as patiently, while he tried over and over to get the engine to start. At length, his hat pushed to the back of his head, his coat off and his sleeves rolled up, he ordered us all out. He thought he knew what was wrong, but he'd have to get the car into the village to the mechanic on Main Street to get it fixed. Uncle John managed to get the car hitched to the tractor and away they went, Uncle John on the tractor and Aunt Lydia steering the Chev.

We were disappointed, of course. Now we wouldn't be able to leave until after lunch. We would have to have our picnic around the kitchen table. Nevertheless, it was a fine day and Corny and I got out his old bicycle for me and his new one for him.

The wind was raw, especially when clouds scudded across the sun. With my pleated skirt bunched under me on the bicycle seat, we set out along the dirt road that hugged the lake. I sped ahead of Corny. "Wait up," he cried. "Where are we going?" I knew, but I wouldn't tell him.

Before long we had rounded one shore of the lake and soon saw the stone gateposts and the stone house. I stopped.

Corny pulled up behind me. "What are you doing?" he said. "You're not supposed to be here. Remember?"

"I know," I said. "And I won't come ever again. But there's something I have to do, something I have to get straight."

"What?"

"You wouldn't understand."

We walked our bicycles between the gateposts, looking to left and right, not wanting to be caught unawares by crazy Lucy. No one was about. Smoke trickled meagerly above the chimney. Large chunks of wood lay heaped, waiting to be split and piled near the kitchen door. An ax imbedded in a block of wood invited all comers to take a turn. Corny pumped on the ax handle to free it.

"Come in with me," I said to him.

"Not me. Why should I?" he pouted. "You won't even tell me what it's about." He swung the ax as hard as he could.

I paused, considered telling him, but, in the end, didn't. He would just ask too many questions.

I had trouble keeping my teeth from chattering, although I was wearing a jacket, two sweaters, and long stockings. I stared at the house, arms tight to my chest, knuckles of both wind-roughened hands pressing against my mouth. I approached the entry, a dark space under the eaves, and knocked timidly. Then louder.

The door opened a crack, just wide enough for me to glimpse an eye peering out, and then it slammed in my face. Behind the door I could hear mad Lucy shouting gibberish. I looked back at Corny, beckoning him over, but he was swinging the ax above a thick piece of wood and bringing it down with all his might. His glancing blow produced merely a wood chip. Swearing under his breath, he tried again.

Abruptly, the door swung open and Lucy's slack-featured face bent to mine. "Little pig, little pig, let me come in," she shrieked, and lowered her voice. "No-no, by the hair of my chinny-chin-chin."

"Lucy?" I could hear Great-Aunt Eileen's voice.

"You'll never come in."

"Lucy!" A commanding tone now.

Lucy swooped at me before I could run, and crushing me tightly against her – her long thick hair in my face, suffocating me – she swung me into the kitchen.

The next moment Eileen was there, grappling with her to free me, wheedling, bribing. Lucy relinquished me in favor of the new pencil Eileen offered. She lumbered to the table, sat down, and was soon busy, her face bent closely over a sheet of paper.

"Well," Eileen said, "Adele's girl, I declare. Getting to be quite the little gadabout. I've tea on, if you'd like."

Too breathless to speak, I shook my head, scraping at my tongue to rid it of Lucy's smelly hair. I wanted to stay near the door, but remembered from my last visit Eileen's surprising strength. I allowed myself to be led to the table. Sitting very straight, I scraped my chair backwards, an inch at a time, to get as far as possible from Lucy. *How should I begin?* I wondered.

"Mother well?" Eileen asked. Lucy continued to sit, head down, pencil busy.

"Yes."

"Sisters all well?"

I nodded, deciding to get right to the point. "Would . . . would you say Great-Aunt Nell was . . . was . . . not in her right mind, that time I was here before?"

"Brighter than she'd been in days, she was. Lucid as the dawn."

I tried again. "Wh-why did she pick me to be the one? Why couldn't one of my sisters just as easily be our great-grandmother all over again?"

"Because of your place in the family, of course, girlie. Your mother was a seventh daughter and you are her seventh daughter. That's how it works, pet. Seventh daughter of a seventh daughter. You can't change that."

"Well, then, she made a mistake, didn't she?" My voice was prim, Miss Goody Two-shoes.

"Did she?"

"Yes." Still prim. "I'm not the seventh daughter."

"Yes, you are."

Big hollow drum *boom-boom*ing inside me. I searched the old woman's square face, looking for the teasing, the joke. Eileen's eyes peered back, one half-closed. "I beg your pardon?" My voice was icy, now, scathingly polite. "I'm afraid you are mistaken. I have only five sisters; I am the sixth."

"No, my dear, you have six sisters; you are the seventh."

My cheeks burned. I had never been faced with such a brazen lie from an adult. My mouth hung open in dismay. I wanted to burst into tears and scream, "Take that back. No fair! I'm only a child."

"That's a lie!" I said. If this woman could be loathsome, I could be rude. "I guess I should know how many sisters I have!"

Eileen sat, hands folded, looking calmly at me, her wide chest heaving up and down. Lucy kept herself hunched away from us, never looking up from her drawing. "I wouldn't worry your head about it," Eileen said. "It's not important enough for you to rile yourself over." Her eyes rested on me sympathetically.

"Why did you say I have six sisters?"

"The truth is best looked at from more than one side, or not at all."

I frowned. This made absolutely no sense. I strained then to catch a glimpse of Lucy's drawing, but couldn't. Lucy held the pencil clumsily and seemed to be making little scratch marks, which is about all you'd expect from somebody like that. A lunatic. A houseful of lunatics.

"I have to go, now," I said. "I just wanted to let you know that our family doesn't believe in fortune-telling, or in any of the hocus-pocus that goes along with it."

Eileen heaved a noisy disgruntled sigh and shrugged. *She knows I have the better of her.* I stood up, feeling lighter, freer. I had settled something once and for all.

"Lucy," Eileen said. "Show us your picture before the girl leaves." Lucy grunted something. She kept on scratching at her paper. I stood waiting, thinking this ought to be good for a laugh.

In a moment, Lucy slid the paper toward Eileen and leaned on her elbow on the table, facing away from us. Eileen glanced at the paper and handed it to me. I looked at it and sat down again, staring in disbelief at a perfect likeness of myself looking terrified, peeping through a half-closed door. It was detailed and almost photographically accurate.

"How . . . ?" I began. "How did she do that?" I stared at the back of Lucy's head, in wonder. "How come she's so . . . good?"

"She's always been good. Why, she has enough pictures to open an art gallery. Lucy," Eileen said. "Who's this a picture of?"

Lucy squeaked a nervous giggle.

"Who?" Eileen repeated. "Tell us."

"Little pig," Lucy said, with a snuffling giggle.

"Who?" Eileen insisted.

"Little pig, little pig," Lucy laughed. "Little sister."

I was perched on the edge of the chair, my back board-straight, gaping at the mad woman who had begun to rock back and forth over her knees, patting her mouth. My skin felt like prickly heat, burning, tingling. Tears flew into my eyes. "No!" I tried to say, but my mouth was too dry. Eileen reached out to pat my hand, but I pulled back. "That's not true," I was able to whisper. "How could it be?"

"These things happen," Eileen said. "They just happen. Your mother tried to look after her, bless her, but she hadn't the strength, or the courage, and then more babies came and well, Nell and I had no one ourselves and said we'd take her, give her a home, watch out for her." She gestured with palms up. "We did what we could. What'll become of her when I go, I don't know. Adele will have to come up with something."

My ability to think, and even to speak in a normal voice, slowly returned. "Do my sisters know about her?"

"Doubt Adele's told them. She'll have to, sooner or later. Arrangements will have to be made. I'm getting on. Adele, herself, is getting on. It may fall upon you girls to look after your sister."

I shuddered. I would never think of this foul, bedraggled half-animal as my sister. I had to leave; my legs ached to run away from this grotesque creature. I stood up hastily, knocking my chair over.

Lucy was beside me in a flash, shoving the picture at me, pressing it against my chest.

I backed away from it. "I don't want it!" I screamed.

"You take!" Lucy growled back. She had her hand up, threatening me with a wallop. I clutched the picture, whimpering, and backed up to the door. Eileen put a restraining hand on Lucy's arm and guided her back to the table. I turned and fled.

Corny was still swinging the ax in the general direction of a piece of firewood. Quickly I folded and refolded the picture, until it was a small wad, and thrust it up the sleeve of my sweater. "Come on!" I yelled, picking up one of the bicycles. "Let's go!"

"Wait'll I stack the wood," he called.

"Can't!" I yelled, and took off down the road without him.

I pedaled hard to get some distance between myself and the stone house, all the while thinking, *What am I going to do? I'm a seventh daughter.* Unless it was a big lie. But it wasn't a lie; I began to see that. Lucy, monstrous though she was, shared certain family characteristics – my mother's and Marietta's straight eyebrows, Beatrice's high cheekbones, Vanessa's snub nose. Yet, it was unthinkable, worse than a nightmare because there was no way to wake up.

My head was ready to burst with the jumble of questions roiling inside my brain. *Was I a witch? Could I enchant people? Was I able to see the future? Was it all an old wives' tale? How would I know?* I was pedaling hard up a long hill, panting, sweating, arguing with myself. *You don't have to believe it. It's baloney, a made-up story.*

I got off to walk to the top and thought, if it's true, maybe I could take up telling fortunes. What if it really *was* true! It could be kind of fun, especially at school. I could tell all the kids what marks they were going to get, or what they were getting for Christmas or their birthdays. I could tell them who was going to get into the school play. I thought hard about the play, but was none the wiser. There was no stage-lit sign in the air with a cast list on it. I got back on the bike and coasted down the other side of the hill.

8

I remembered almost nothing about our trip to the United States. Corny kept telling me I was no fun, that all I wanted to do was sulk. I wasn't sulking, though. I was trying to read the future, but it wasn't working. I *do* remember being disappointed by the countryside. It looked pretty much like our own. Uncle John's sister, in spite of being sick with something called shingles, looked like us, except she looked tired and had blotches on her face. She *did* have a different way of talking, kind of slangy with skinny vowels. She was real glad to see us, she said, whereas the Merricks were really glad to see her. I was pretty neutral about the gladness, mainly because I was trying to see whether I was clairvoyant even in the United States. Apparently, I wasn't. Maybe I needed some sort of shortwave connection.

Once back in Canada, though, I thought I was actually getting the hang of it. I said to the back of Uncle John's head, "It's going to rain."

"Yes, I expect you're right. Those clouds must mean something."

"No, but, I *know* it's going to rain."

"Sure smells like rain."

About fifteen minutes later, the sun peeked through the clouds and threatened to vanquish them altogether. *Well, that settles it,* I thought. It was all a big stupid lie. I could no more see into the future than read the label on the neck of my sweater.

Botany wool. Child's medium.

Huh? I almost said out loud. *Is that really what it said?* Maybe I *was* clairvoyant. On the other hand, how many times must I have seen that label taking off my sweater, turning it right-side-out, putting it on?

"Corny, could you look at the label on my sweater and see what it says?"

"Why?"

"Just do it."

He grabbed the neck of my sweater and pulled it closer to him, while I nearly strangled. "Bot-an-y wool, child's med.," he read. I nodded, pleased, and pulled my sweater out of his clutches. *It's possible,* I thought, smiling. I was imagining the kids at school and how they would all make a big fuss over me because I had this magic talent.

The Merricks drove me straight home. They came in to tell Adele all about the trip, and were invited to stay for supper. I thought about what we might be having. *Roast chicken.* I loved roast chicken. Corny and I went outside to throw a ball around. "What do you bet we're having for supper?" I said.

"Meatloaf and baked potatoes."

"Nope, roast chicken."

"Nope, meatloaf."

"Shows how much you know. It's roast chicken."

"Betcha a nickel."

"Okay, sure, a nickel it is."

We were soon called in to wash our hands and sit down to a large family-sized meatloaf, a dish full of baked potatoes, and a spoonful each of colorless canned peas. With a not particularly gracious sigh, I handed my nickel over to Corny. "What made you think meatloaf?" I asked him later. *Could he somehow be horning in on my clairvoyance? How unfair.*

"I looked in the oven."

Back at school after the weekend, I was hoping to be able to put my talent to the test. A rumor was going around that the police had found some stuff belonging to Faye Wirt. And sure enough, a few days later a policeman came into our classroom to have a little talk with us. "Does anybody recognize this jacket?" he asked us.

Nearly all the girls put up their hands, and even a couple of the boys. "It's Faye's," Carol Ann Hagen said, and everyone nodded. I didn't, because, as a matter of fact, I thought it was Vanessa's. At least, she had one sort of like it.

The police also had found a blanket, some candles, and a notebook. It turned out that Faye had a little hideout, inside an old wooden boxcar that had been pushed off the track and rolled down behind the baggage shed at the station. The policeman asked if any of us knew about this place.

Carol Ann and a couple of other girls put up their hands. "It's where she used to hide from her father," Carol Ann said. "She's been murdered, hasn't she?"

The policeman didn't actually answer her question, but you could tell by the look on his face that that's what he thought. After he left, everybody started talking at once and Miss Boyle let them. The bigger girls were crying and saying things like, "I just knew this was going to happen."

"I can't believe her own father would kill her."

"I can. I knew she wouldn't run away."

"Well, I figured all along that's what happened."

When they finally stopped talking about what a great kid she was, and what a horrible monster her father was, I said quietly, "But she's not dead."

At first there was silence. Then everybody talked at once, telling me I was an idiot; that I didn't know anything; that I should smarten up; that maybe I was mixed up in it, too. Maybe I was an accomplice because, after all, she and I never did get along.

At home, Sylvia and Cynthia said they had heard a rumor that they were going to lock up Faye's father on suspicion of murder because they found her diary. "She said right in it that she was afraid her father was going to kill her," Sylvia said.

"But he didn't kill her," I said.

"Then who did?"

"Nobody. She's not dead."

Sylvia shook her head at me in this knowing way she has, and Cynthia patted me on the shoulder. "It's all right," she said. "We're all entitled to our own opinions."

About a week later, it was in the paper that a "quantity of blood" had been found inside the boxcar and that Mr. Wirt was under arrest for suspicion of murder. At school, Carol Ann said, "Not as smart as you think you are, pip-squeak! Do you believe it now?" All I could do was shrug.

So, I didn't have second sight, after all. I should have been relieved. And, in a way, I was. But, still, something nagged away at the back of my mind.

After school I went home, but even though it had begun to sprinkle rain, I didn't go inside. Instead I went around the side of the house and into the back garden. I squeezed through the broken part of the fence into the woodlot behind, searching for the tree where I'd hidden the barrette. I couldn't find it. I would have looked further, but it was beginning to pour.

I was confused.

Next day at school, I couldn't stop thinking about it. If I had this supposed gift, why didn't it work all the time? I should have been able to see the marks on the test papers Miss Boyle was handing back, but I couldn't. I no longer knew what to believe about the state of my mind. I tried thinking about other things. I tried thinking about nothing.

And then something happened.

"Now then, class," Miss Boyle announced on Friday afternoon, "I have a surprise for you." I stared hard at her, but had no idea what the surprise would be. "Some lucky young people are going to have their artwork displayed in the town hall. You will each produce a picture to be judged by the mayor. The top three will win five dollars, and the best overall will also receive a medal. Take out your art pads. You may begin."

I sat with a blank page in front of me and my drawing pencil clutched firmly, knowing what I wanted to draw, but unable to start. I would not draw my usual caricatures, my monstrous people. I wanted to produce a scene of such great beauty that the mayor would be in awe. I forced myself to start in the bottom right corner with some grass, tufts of grass, a few individual blades, some rocks almost buried in the grass, a head lying on them. *Oops. No.* Not what I had meant to do at all. I managed to erase the head, most of it anyway, and left the grass for later. I would draw a tree. Large, bent trunk, thick branches, leaves just coming out. It was our climbing tree, in the forest behind our house.

"Very nice," Miss Boyle said, as she strolled past my desk. I smiled sweetly, warmed by the praise she so seldom bestowed on me.

I found that I was drawing rocks under the tree again and a person lying on them. I tried erasing again, but the outline was still there. This was silly. Maybe I was so used to drawing people that my hand just automatically did it. I was kind of scaring myself. I got out my paints and brushed delicate yellowish green bladelike strokes over the person lying there. I tackled the tree again and filled in some pale new leafy foliage, except where there was the jagged edge of a broken branch. *I should have done the sky first,* I thought, as I tried patching in bits of sky behind the tree.

"Wait a minute. There's no broken branch," I said out loud.

"No talking, class. You should be concentrating on your pictures."

I hated this picture. It was terrible. I was no good at drawing scenes. I crumpled it up and marched with it to the front of the class, where I deposited it in the large metal wastebasket.

"You have only ten minutes left, Rosalind. If you wish to enter the competition, you will have to work quickly."

I wasn't really sure that I *did* want to enter the competition. I got out another sheet of paper and began in the very center with the drawing of an eye. Behind my eyes, I could feel a headache coming on. Around the eye I drew a circle, and around that another circle, until, moving my drawing pencil faster and faster round and round the paper, I had filled it with gray-black circles. My head throbbed.

Miss Boyle was gathering the pictures. Some she would hold up to show the class, with comments like "a perfect house," or, "a good attempt at a horse," or, "a very commendable army jeep." She picked up mine and said, "Whatever possessed you to do this? A child's scribbles." She didn't hold it up. I couldn't even shrug. I just sat as still as possible, trying to keep my head from bursting apart.

After school, I headed for home – alone, as usual. Carol Ann and a couple of other kids called after me, "Hey, Scribbles, think you'll win the medal?" That's when I ran, in spite of my headache. I didn't care who was going to win.

Saturday was sunny and almost warm. Both Marietta and Vanessa were home for the weekend. The twins confessed to having spring fever and urged us all to go into the woods after lunch to see how it had fared over the winter.

"Coming with us, Ros?" Marietta called up the stairs. In my room, I put away the notebook I now used for my drawings. I had run out of wallpaper rolls. I hadn't really been drawing in it, merely doodling – brushing my soft pencil back and forth, making a widening furry wedge like the reverse of a windshield wiper, covering up space instead of clearing it.

I didn't feel well. I still had a headache and I'd had a pain in my stomach all morning that came and went and made me feel slow and stupid. Maybe a walk in the fresh air would help.

I trailed them through the grass, green where the sun could reach it; winter pale, still, near the roots of trees. Vanessa, romping ahead of everyone, dragged open the broken section of board fencing at the back of the garden, and they all crept through into the woodlot. I stopped. My chest felt tight. My breathing was quick and shallow. I was sweating so much, it stung my eyes. *We shouldn't be doing this,* I thought. *Warn them.*

I sidled through the gap in the fence. They were way ahead, laughing hilariously at something Vanessa had said. "Hurry up," Marietta called to me. I took a deep breath.

This is silly. We've done this all our lives, I told myself. We had always loved this place, even though Adele kept threatening to sell it. "It's spongy in the spring, it's alive with mosquitoes in summer, and treacherous underfoot in winter. What good is it?" she'd say. But she never could quite reconcile herself to having neighbors so close. You could go back there and be hidden completely from the world.

Nothing was wrong. By the time I reached the pond, I had convinced myself that I felt better. Marietta, Vanessa, and I had taught ourselves to swim in this spring-fed pond, while Beatrice and the twins, none of whom could swim a stroke, supervised. If any of us drowned, the twins were supposed to run to the house for help and Bea would stay and watch, I guess.

Ahead was the climbing tree, a deformed and ancient maple that we sometimes called the Aeroplane, sometimes the Castle, and sometimes the Elephant. Even though my sisters were too grown-up to play in a tree, its bent trunk was an irresistible invitation to climb. Thick and gnarled in old age, the elephantine trunk formed a ramp, allowing easy access to the spreading branches that took off from the main body of the tree in clusters, like the spread wings of a flying ship, or the buttresses and lookouts of a fortress.

Even at her age, Marietta liked to revert to childhood when she came home. "Come on up," she called, clambering easily up the slanted trunk, reaching for a branch to steady herself. I stood underneath, trying to smile away a bout of dizziness. The twins followed, giving each other a boost and a hand up, and soon settled into the cockpit of the sky clipper. Marietta was by now high in the elephant's howdah, surveying her empire, which left the castle for Vanessa and no place in particular for me.

Marietta called down, "Come on, there's room on the elephant's back for two." And there was, I could see that, but still I stood where I was. Vanessa, the last one to crawl up, clung to an overhead branch, looking for her next foothold.

"Someone's going to fall!" I called. I knew this now. I think I had known it since yesterday in school, working on my drawing. I should have warned them, prevented them from doing this. It would be Vanessa, I was positive.

Vanessa yelled, "Don't be a sissy!" The twins were encouraging Vanessa up to the next level.

"Vanessa, don't go!" I shrieked. "You're going to fall!" I

could feel the rush of air, the panic, the blur of branches, the sharp screaming pain. And then the dark.

Vanessa found her foothold and moved up to the next cluster of branches. Gripping the sturdiest, she peered at me. "Don't be such a worrywart."

In her howdah, I could see Marietta looking down uneasily. "Everybody's fine, Ros. Come on up."

Feeling stupid and dizzy and heavy, I turned away. I couldn't bear to watch. I retraced my steps through the underbrush, fighting off clawing branches of wild raspberry, tripping over cedar roots. A young poplar slapped at my face. When I reached the broken part of the fence at the end of the garden, I ran toward the house, letting the kitchen door slam behind me.

Within minutes the kitchen door slammed behind Marietta as she ran through the house calling out, "Vanessa's fallen out of the tree. I'm calling for the ambulance."

Adele came running. "Ambulance! Dear God! How bad is she?"

Hours passed. Our mother and Marietta were still at the hospital with Vanessa. At home, the twins and I slouched around the house, following each other from sitting room to kitchen and back again. "How did you know she was going to fall?" Sylvia asked me. I just shrugged. "No, but you knew. How come?"

"I don't know how I knew, I just knew." This wasn't good enough for either me *or* Sylvia. She kept at me, insisting that I must have seen something; must have known something from the last time I climbed the tree; must have. . . .

Cynthia finally said to her, "I think you should stop. She doesn't know. There are times when you just don't know something." I was grateful for Cynthia's support, but it didn't make matters any better. I went up to my room to think. I knew that I had had a premonition, yet it felt so vague that I hadn't really understood what it was until it was too late. I hadn't been paying enough attention to it. It was my fault that Vanessa fell. I should have blocked her path, wrestled with her, sat on her, or at least tried to catch her as she fell. Instead, I ran away. A coward.

Cynthia phoned Beatrice to tell her what had happened. Bea wondered if she should come home, although given her condition, she probably shouldn't. Cynthia didn't know. "Mother will call you," she said.

Marietta, reluctantly, took the train back on Monday to the hospital where she was interning. With Vanessa in a coma, there was really very little she, or anyone, could do. For the next three weeks, Adele practically lived at the hospital, setting off grimly in the morning and returning at supper time, her face a mask revealing nothing of how she felt.

At first I went after school each day. I was allowed into Vanessa's stark room to stare at her lying in her hospital bed, the sides up, a tube from her arm attached to a bottle of fluid hanging from a tall stand. Her other arm was in plaster. Her eyes were closed. She's just asleep, I told myself, but she looked dead.

Adele was always there when I was, but one day, about a week after the accident, she left the room for a few minutes. When she had gone, I touched Vanessa's fingers, curled loosely around the edge of her plaster cast, and whispered, "Please don't die, Vanessa. Please wake up. It's my fault. I'm sorry, I'm really sorry." There had to be something else to say, something I could do to bring her back, but I couldn't think what, and so I just kept whispering, "I'm sorry."

At home, we moved slowly through our lives. No one smiled. No one could think of anything much to say. Bea came home on the train and stayed for a week. Marietta came when she could. It was as if we were each drifting in and out of our own personal coma.

When I wasn't at school or at the hospital, I stayed in my room, furiously drawing pictures of ghoulish figures – monsters, fiends dripping blood from their fingernails, tormented creatures burning in hellfires. I wanted to jab something sharp into my skin, but I couldn't bring myself to do it.

Adele phoned the secretarial school and explained. Then she phoned the boardinghouse where many of the girls from out of town lived. Our phone rang constantly, with Vanessa's friends wanting news.

I was at the hospital with Adele when a grave-looking specialist, shaking his head, came out of Vanessa's room. That night I couldn't stop crying. Adele sat on the edge of the bed and took my hand. "What will be, will be, Rosalind. You must know that." She looked into my eyes, swimming with tears, and squeezed my hand. "It was an accident," she said. "Why you continue to blame yourself, I do not know."

Didn't she really? Could she so easily ignore what the old aunts believed to be true about her own grandmother and about me? Perhaps there was a way for me to see only what I wanted to see. Maybe I could learn to believe only what I wanted to believe. I didn't know if it was possible; I just knew I had to do something.

Trees were definitely in bud now; some even had tiny leaves. It was nearly Easter. One day at school, just before recess while I was trying to finish my arithmetic problems, I thought I heard a little sigh, or perhaps a whisper. I thought someone behind me said something like, "It's all right," or, "All is right," or maybe it was nothing. I turned around, thinking for some reason of Faye, but of course, her desk was empty. Still, a certain heaviness had disappeared from my head. I was anxious to get home.

That evening Adele returned from the hospital and sat down at the table, where the twins and I were just serving a casserole Adele had made earlier in the day. Sylvia put some on a plate for Adele. She stared at it, then pushed it aside, and with elbows resting on the table, she wept into her hands.

My heart boomed hollowly; hair on my arms stood on end. I had thought Vanessa might be taking a turn for the better. I had had what I thought was a premonition – clearly a wrong one. It seemed that I couldn't count on anything.

"Mother?" I said, pulling a hand away from her face. "Is she worse?"

Adele looked up at us, her tear-streaked face lined and puffy. "They think she's going to be all right. I'm sorry, I can't help crying. I've held back my tears for so long."

CHAPTER

9

Vanessa was at last permitted to come home. Although she had regained consciousness, she sounded vague and tired, as if she'd been on a long arduous journey. Her head was no longer bandaged, but her arm was still in plaster. She remembered almost nothing about falling out of the tree. I sat with her each afternoon after school, sometimes reading aloud to her, or just sitting, clenching and unclenching my hands, watching her look out the window.

"I tried to warn you," I said finally, when I could no longer stand not talking about it.

"Mmm?" she said, as if her thoughts had been far away.

I repeated what I'd said. "But you wouldn't listen. Maybe I should have done more . . . done something to convince you."

"I don't remember," she said. "I think I fell."

"I knew you were going to. Maybe I could have stopped you."

She looked at me now, her eyes more focused than they had been. Adele came into the room to put a hand on Vanessa's forehead.

"Ros knew I was going to fall," she said to our mother. "Did you notice a rotten branch?"

"No, I just knew." My eyes were downcast.

Adele said, "Come downstairs, now, Rosalind, and let your sister rest."

Vanessa said, "But she knew I was going to fall."

"Don't be foolish!" Adele said, straightening Vanessa's pillow. "Someone was bound to fall out of that blasted tree, sooner or later. And you're such a daredevil, Vanessa! I might have known it would be you."

"I don't feel well," I said after dinner. I had eaten almost nothing.

Adele looked at me sharply. "Stomachache?" she asked.

I shrugged.

"Stomach cramps?"

"Maybe." It felt like whatever it had been a month ago – the day of Vanessa's accident.

With a knowing eye, Adele said, "I think an early night will do you a world of good. Off to bed you go, and I'll be up to see how you are in a few minutes."

When she came up, she sat on the end of my bed and talked of things I didn't want to hear. Growing up. My body changing into the body of a woman. Cramps. Blood.

I hated what she was saying. My frame was narrow, sprightly. Why would I want to change it for the bulges of a woman? Why hadn't I been born a boy? Boys were so care-free, so well equipped for real life, their clothes so sensible. If I was soon to be a woman, how would that affect this busi-ness I seemed to have inherited of telling the future? *Could it get worse?* Foretelling Vanessa's fall from the tree was bad enough. Having no one listen to me made me feel helpless. And hopeless. If that was an example of girls' intuition, I didn't want to grow into a woman.

The very word *blood* made my skin crawl. I had got through the gashes and scrapes of childhood without much bloodshed. "Be a brave little soldier," Adele used to tell me. I had always been able to stop up a cut finger or a scraped knee by staying completely still and concentrating. That was what *brave* meant, I had thought. "Go away," I wanted to say to her. "Just tuck me in and turn out the light."

Instead, I watched Adele stare vacantly at a nursery picture on the wall of a row of children waiting for a train. She straightened it and said, "I think it's time you and I had a little talk about things the old aunts might have told you." Although Great-Aunt Nell had died shortly after my visit, everything about her remained in my mind – her faltering voice, her red-rimmed eyes, her translucent skin.

"I'm pretty tired."

"My aunts made predictions about you, didn't they?" She looked at me fiercely, ignoring my exaggerated yawn.

"I don't remember." I pulled the covers up to my chin,

but she waited, wanting an answer. "It was just something stupid. Like something you'd read."

"Exactly. It's balderdash. Evil old crones! Sixth sense, my foot! Your great-grandmother no more had sixth sense than I have two heads. We know, nowadays, that it just isn't possible. If she told fortunes, and apparently she did, she may well have told people exactly what they wanted to hear. She may have listened very closely to what they said about themselves and gleaned information about them that way. She was probably a good judge of character."

Adele's mood brightened as she convinced herself that I had not foreseen Vanessa's fall. While she talked, I concentrated on one thing. Lying snugly in bed, Adele droning on and on about possibilities and impossibilities, the known world and the unknown, the fine line between logic and fairy tales, I trained my mind inwards, deep inside a tunnel, remaining there for a very long time, filling the emptiness, until I knew it was safe to emerge.

"No one can know what will happen in the future," Adele said. "If a person could, it would be all over the front page of all the newspapers, wouldn't it? If your great-grandmother could truly predict the future, why did she charge only twenty-five cents? Why didn't she move to the city and make a fortune for herself? I expect her teacup readings were worth exactly what she charged and she was shrewd enough to know that.

"You're at a very suggestible age, Rosalind. Strange things happen, sometimes, when you are at the point of growing up.

The fact that you sensed that something terrible was going to happen doesn't mean anything. Not a thing. Why, if I had been watching you girls in the tree, I'd have been afraid, too. Any one of you might have fallen. Reasonable people don't put any stock in telling the future. It's not logical. It doesn't fit with what we know about the world and about ourselves. What you were experiencing was very likely related to the fact that you are becoming a young woman."

It was my mother who wasn't making sense.

I spent Good Friday thinking about my predicament and finally reached a conclusion: I couldn't live the rest of my life foretelling horrible things. I couldn't go on as I was, a seventh daughter of a seventh daughter. Something had to change. And I was beginning to see what that was.

Next morning I went downstairs toward the smell of fresh coffee and sizzling bacon, sauntering into the kitchen as if nothing much was up. I avoided Adele's eyes. "I want to spend some of the holiday out on the farm with Corny."

Adele, heavy-eyed, turned from the bacon sputtering in the frying pan and studied me as if she sensed a change – an excitement I was having trouble concealing. She turned the bacon. "I think you'd be wiser to stay home."

"No, I want to talk to Corny. I want to see if the barn cat had her kittens. It will be good for me."

Adele made a noncommittal sound.

"I really want to go."

She sighed. "If I say no, you'll just keep it up and keep it up until I give in, so I might as well save myself a long battle that I haven't the strength to fight. I'll phone and ask Lydia if she feels like having you. Now, eat your breakfast."

Adele turned haggard eyes on me from time to time. She looked exhausted. The twins wandered into the kitchen, helping themselves to bacon and toast.

Following breakfast, Adele called Aunt Lydia. She had to shout because Lydia's party-line connection was so poor. Adele had to repeat her request three times before Lydia could properly make it out.

"Don't put her on the train. John's going to town this morning and can pick her up."

Uncle John and I got to the farm in time for lunch. Afterwards, Corny and I got out the bikes. While we rode along side by side, I watched him, taking note of his boyishness. He made a big snuffling sound with his nose, hawked, and spat over his shoulder. I tried to do the same, but spit dribbled disgustingly down the sleeve of my sweater. I steered with one hand while I flicked it off. When we got back to the barn, where the bikes were stored, Corny dismounted gracefully, throwing his leg over the seat and back wheel. I tried it, got hung up on my skirt, and fell with the bike in a heap.

"El Stupido," Corny said.

"Shut up!" I yelled. I stomped into the house, up the stairs, and slammed the door of the guest room behind me. Soon I could hear Corny breathing on the other side of the door.

"What's wrong, Ros?" he whispered, sounding worried. When I didn't answer, he pushed the door open and stood there.

I was sitting in the middle of the bed, cross-legged. At length I said, "I want to be a boy."

Corny frowned and then shrugged, not seeming the least bit surprised. He was a boy, boys were enviable. He'd made me aware of that often enough.

Aunt Lydia appeared on the stairs. "What's wrong with Rosalind?"

Corny said, "She wishes she was a boy."

Oh, thanks, Corny, I thought. *Nice going.*

In a moment, Aunt Lydia was in the room. "Now, what's all this about?" she asked.

"My life is horrible. I hate myself." I started to cry.

"Now, now. It can't be that bad." She shooed Corny out.

I lay on the bed, face buried on my arms. Lydia rubbed my back. "You're just at that awkward stage," she said, "surrounded by all of life's little mysteries. You'll live through it. We all do."

"No, I won't," I said.

Lydia just laughed. I stopped crying, and soon Lydia left to go back down to her ironing, leaving the bedroom door open. I rolled onto my back. I wasn't going to live through "it" because I'd stopped "it" through sheer willpower. If I could do that, surely the possibilities were endless.

Corny was in the doorway, again. "You have to help me become a boy," I said.

He frowned, not just sure if I was playing a game. He thought about what was at stake. "You'd have to cut your hair, you know."

"I know."

I got off the bed and stood in front of him.

Appraising me, he took in my brown Oxfords, white kneesocks stained with bicycle grease, pleated plaid skirt, and white blouse, a hand-me-down – one of two, in fact, from the twins, and now a bit tight across my chest.

I watched his eyes move slowly from the floor upwards, and then stop at chest level. Our eyes met. I half-closed mine in a threat that said clearly, *Make a remark on pain of death*. Corny understood perfectly. He looked away without comment, blushing furiously.

"I want you to give me some clothes," I said.

I watched his expression change from puzzled to excited by what I was about to do. He beckoned me to follow him into his room. There, he ransacked his closet and a chest of drawers and came up with an old pair of knee breeches, now a little too small for him, trousers, two shirts, two ties. He insisted on two. And finally, kneesocks and a wonderful pair of boots, with a big hole coming in the sole of one.

10

It probably sounds stupid – a twelve-year-old girl trying to pass herself off as a boy. The thing is, though, I was kind of thinking about Corny and his birthmark that looks for all the world like raw beefsteak smeared over half his face. As far as he's concerned, unless he's confronted with a mirror, both sides of his face look just fine. Therefore (I know there's no connection, but it doesn't matter), if I dressed like a boy, and acted like a boy, then I could believe that I was no longer a girl – no longer a seventh daughter of a seventh daughter.

Well, it made sense to me, anyway.

For twelve years, I had believed that everything was exactly what it seemed. I believed that I was me, the same me I would be forever. I had also believed that I had only five sisters. Now, I knew that nothing was what it seemed. My life was changed, my body changing, and on top of this, I somehow had been singled out to see things before they happened. This was not a gift; it was a burden. But I was going to do something about it. If I could manage one more change, I could escape it. I held Corny's shirt up to me and looked in the mirror on the dresser. If Corny could make-believe that by turning his head he could make his face look normal, then I could do something like it. It would take a lot of effort, but if I believed in what I was about to do, and kept believing, it might work. It might set me free.

Back in the guest room, I unbuttoned my skirt, let it fall to the floor, and stepped out of it. I squirmed out of my blouse. I wrenched off my petticoat. Unshackled, I stood in my sensible underpants and sleeveless undershirt, and knew that giving up my girlhood would be easy. I could happily give up puffed sleeves, woolly over-drawers, sweat-inducing taffeta for parties, my hair scraped into braids, a lineup of dolls too good to play with, tripping over the skipping ropes in double Dutch. My winter boots. I thought about my velvety boots, with fur around the top and down the front. I might regret those, although I didn't mind a bit replacing my skirt with trousers I could wear every day, even to school. I pulled them on and felt their roughness against the soft skin of the insides of my thighs. I felt like standing with my legs apart. The buttons in front were awkward to do up. Corny had neglected to give me either suspenders or a belt. I pulled the shirt on, fumbling with the buttons, placed, for some reason, on the wrong side. I tucked it in, bunching it up at the waist to hold the trousers up.

Hands deep in my pockets, I stood in front of the chipped mirror on the wall behind the door. The trousers were gray tweed. The shirt was blue with dark blue checks, and looked pretty good – baggy, carefree. I undid the ribbons binding my braids and shook out my hair. It stood out from my head like a crimped lamp shade. I walked back and forth past the mirror, glancing in now and then, but felt oddly off balance walking with both hands in my pockets.

I took a breath, opened the door, and stepped out, newly masculine. Corny was waiting for me in the hall. Aunt Lydia was trudging up the stairs with a pile of freshly ironed clothes. Watching his mother's head rise high enough to catch a view of me through the balustrade, Corny began to whistle. He leaned against the wall, hands in his pockets, and whistled through his teeth at the ceiling. I stood still and bit my lip.

"What game is this?" Aunt Lydia asked, wide-eyed at sight of me.

"Corny gave me some clothes," I said, wanting to ease into divulging my gender change.

"Did he indeed! Not those good trousers, I hope. Straight out of Eaton's catalogue and they're to see him through this entire year."

"I don't want them," Corny said. "At school they call me fancy-pants behind my back. I hate it."

"How do you know what they say, if it's behind your back?"

He looked at his mother and away. "You always know."

"May I have them?" I begged.

"Oh, my, dear, no," Aunt Lydia said. "Not those. They're far too good."

I guess Lydia just couldn't bear to see those trousers walk away. I don't think it was so much because they were expensive. I actually think it was because she had such high hopes for her son. Maybe she figured that Cornelius would become an important figure in history, and that his trousers were destined for a museum.

Aunt Lydia went back downstairs to speak to Uncle John about the trousers situation. I followed right behind and looked up hopefully at Uncle John. He gazed at me with a distracted grin and a cough to hide his smile.

"Well," he said, at length, "what difference does it make in the long run? There's worse things than dressing up in trousers. Her mother will be happy she's not painting her face and hanging around the dance halls."

"There's no dance hall in Kempton Mills," Aunt Lydia said, sounding peeved.

"Well . . ."

"But they're Eaton's best quality," she tried to reason.

"But if the lad won't wear them, and I can't say I blame him. . . ."

In the end, I got to keep them, as well as two sweaters destined for the church rummage sale, the shirts, ties, and the breeches.

On Sunday, after church (to which I wore my own clothes) and after our noon meal, I told Corny he'd have to help me cut my hair. I changed into his clothes and we took off for our most remote haunt – a plateau of land overlooking an abandoned quarry, about a half hour's walk from the farm. The day was warm. We lay on our stomachs in the long grass, hands under chins, letting our gaze drift down the shelves of limestone layering the walls of the pit.

"I've got the scissors," I said.

Corny rolled over onto his side and leaned on an elbow. He looked at the fair hair partially veiling my face where it hung down over the sleeve of my shirt, formerly his. I propped myself on an elbow, too. I looked him straight in the eye, pushing a hank of hair behind my ear.

He bunched his mouth to one side and shook his head. "I'm not doing it."

I sat up, cross-legged in the itchy pants, the worn soles of my boots on display, and glared. "You have to. You're my best friend. My one and only."

He sat up, wrapped his arms around his knees, and studied my hair. It was fair and silky, unlike his own thick, russet mat that curled when it got long enough to reach his collar. "Your eyes kind of slant down at the corners, you know that?" he said.

"We're not talking about eyes."

"I'm not cutting your hair. They'd kill us."

"They'll get used to it. Please?" I looked into his eyes before he could turn the raw side of his face away. I reached behind me and pulled a small pair of scissors, borrowed from Aunt Lydia's sewing basket, from my hip pocket. Silently, and without releasing him from my gaze, I held them toward him.

Corny was still looking into my eyes, biting hard on his lip. Within his range of vision were the scissors, wobbling as I held them out to him. His eyes wavered from mine, roaming over my lips, nose, ears. He shook his head. "Nope. Not doing it."

He reached out to touch my cheekbone, where my skin felt a little flushed. I pulled back, straightened, rose onto my knees. Corny did the same. I brought the scissors up quickly between us, and he backed off.

"Uh-uh," he said. "N.O." His wavering voice was less sure.

I kept him steadily in my gaze. "If you don't do it, Corny, I will never speak to you again; never look at you; never acknowledge, even, that you exist. You will cease to be my one and only friend."

He took the scissors, his hand trembling.

I shifted closer, sat sideways, and held up a lock of hair. Still on his knees, he grasped a handful and let it fall through his fingers.

"Corny, just do it."

He slipped his hand under another swath of hair, his knuckles rough against my neck, his head bent over mine, and inhaled deeply.

"You don't have to smell it! Just cut it! Cripes flipping Kate, Corny!"

In a moment, my hair fell to the ground. We both looked down and then into each other's startled eyes. "Keep going." My voice was husky with uneasy anticipation of the consequences. For sure, we were going to get slaughtered.

Corny grasped another handful and sawed through it with the scissors.

When the deed was done, there was hair everywhere. A sudden gust of wind blew snippets over the edge of the pit, and we watched them catch on and cling to the naked limestone. We moved away from the remaining feathers. While I shook myself like a dog, Corny brushed them away from his clothes. With one last sad glance at my ragged head, he looked as though he had participated in a death. He handed back the scissors and walked toward his house.

"Wait up!" I called, but he broke into a run.

Aunt Lydia screeched, "Oh, my Lord!" when I came in. Uncle John looked disappointed in me. Corny went up to his room and wouldn't come out. Uncle John drove me home.

Adele was waiting for me at the side door, filling, it seemed, the entire door frame. Lydia had called her, told her everything. Tears, apparently, had been shed. She took one look at me and raised the back of her hand to her forehead, her eyes aimed beseechingly at heaven.

"Go immediately," she said, her voice failing her, "to Miss Edwards'." She took in the breeches, kneesocks, boots; closed her eyes briefly and tightened her lips. "Maybe she can bob that wretched head into some sort of style. At least make it presentable." She held out two quarters for the haircut.

Obediently I reached for the money, but quickly pulled back. I could not give in when I had barely even begun.

"Take it," Adele said crossly. I stared at the money.

I wanted desperately to explain my situation. I wanted to talk about mad Lucy, tell Adele that I knew everything, the whole seventh-daughter thing, and that I chose to escape my fate – that I would not sit quietly and accept things as they were. If being born a seventh daughter had anything to do with seeing disasters, then I meant to fight it. I refused to be a daughter at all. I continued to look up at Adele and saw her grow to huge proportions, filling not only the doorway, but the house, the town we lived in, all the space between earth and sky.

I blurted, "I know all about Lucy. I know who she is." I expected the earth to open and swallow me.

Adele's eyes darkened; color left her cheeks. Her head began to shake, a tremor that seemed to agitate her entire swollen bulk. The whole universe that was my mother trembled, as if she were going to come apart, erupt. But as I watched, her mouth suddenly sagged, empty, out of words. Anger left her eyes, and for a moment they, too, were empty, until something else filled them – the look of someone trapped, found out. Her voice, when it returned, was little more than a whisper. "Look at you! This is raving madness. Surely one lunatic in the family is enough!" She moved from the doorway inside to the kitchen. I followed.

"Do the others know?" I asked.

"Know what?" she said, speaking down from her great height, her voice stronger.

"That Lucy is our sister."

Adele closed her eyes and sat down at the table, head bowed. After a long silence, she said, "Beatrice knows and so does Marietta. I have asked them to keep silent on the topic, and I think they understand. It is the cross I bear, always. The child is well cared for, wants for nothing, cannot be cured. You would do well to learn that things without remedy should be without regard." Adele seemed to gain control of herself as she spoke. Straightening, she said firmly, "I will not have you talking about this, Rosalind, either in this family or to others. I forbid you ever to mention her again. Do you hear me?"

I nodded, at the same time wishing we could go back to being the comfortable family we once had seemed to be, we six girls – our games, our squabbles, our climbing tree, our mother trying to make us appreciate music, wanting us to turn out to be a credit to her.

At the moment, however, it was my transformation that was at issue. "Just answer me this. Why?" Adele's eyes roamed from my hair to my clothes.

I swallowed and said tremulously, "I hate being a girl. I don't want to turn into a woman. And I refuse to be a seventh daughter." There. I'd said it all. I wished my voice could have been stronger, deeper, but it was shrill and girlish.

"Seventh daughter?" Adele said, gazing straight into my eyes, her mouth grim. "Did we not just agree to avoid all reference to Lucy? Did we not agree that what my aunts believe is balderdash?"

"Yes, we did."

"Then kindly stick to your end of the bargain." She sighed deeply and shook her head. She beckoned me to sit, but I couldn't. "When Lucy was born," she said sadly, "she looked barely human. I couldn't stop crying over her and became very ill. As she grew, I was even a little afraid of her, and when more babies came along, your sisters, I feared for them, too. She was so rough, the way she would grab at them and maul them, that Dr. Harmon recommended that I find a home to put her in. Aunt Nell and Aunt Eileen got wind of this, and almost before I knew what had happened, they had swept her up and taken her to live with them in the country. It made such a difference in our lives not to have to be afraid anymore. I felt badly for Lucy, that she had to be taken away from her rightful family, but everyone – my aunts, my sisters, my father, Dr. Harmon, who was just starting out in practice and knew more about modern medicine than he does now, and eventually, even your father – said it was all for the best."

She looked down at her hands and then up at me, where I stood near the door, skinny and clownish in Corny's old clothes, my hair scruffy as a haystack. "Gosh!" was all I could think of to say. I wondered what Adele had been like all those years ago. And Lucy? I could not imagine a murderous toddler.

"Yes, well, there you have it. Now you know."

I nodded and shrugged at the same time, knowing something, but not everything.

"Now, the best thing for you would be to get out of those dreadful clothes, put on something decent, and go downtown to Miss Edwards' hairdressing salon."

"I can't," I said, looking at the floor.

Adele snorted, "*Puh!* As if hacking off your hair and wearing pants could make a particle of difference!"

"You were able to believe you had only six daughters," I accused her.

She stood up, angry now. "Just you get yourself down to Miss Edwards', and hope that she's still open. Quickly! I'm on the verge of collapse."

I took the money and walked slowly down the hill toward Bridge Street, the main thoroughfare, where Miss Edwards had her small beauty parlor. I turned away from the few people I met, feeling their eyes on my head. Across the wide main street, shaded by a thick elm, was Vincent's Barbershop.

I crossed the street. The tree's roots bulged up through the sidewalk, providing a convenient sitting and thinking spot. I squatted and picked at bits of the concrete sidewalk at my feet, broken up by the gnarled root of a single living tree. A woman walking past said hello there, but I ignored her.

I had to make a choice – that much was clear. If I disobeyed my mother, who knew what she might do? She had given away one child; would she send me away, too, to live with Lucy and Great-Aunt Eileen? I would run away first. Like Faye Wirt.

Yet, if I didn't disobey her, if I just let fate rule my life, I might be in constant torment. As Rosalind Kemp, I knew now that I saw too far into things that I could do nothing about. On the other hand, if I could convince myself that I was . . . Ross Kemp, let's say, he would see nothing. I didn't know whether I could fool fate, but I needed to try.

Vincent, the barber, was smoking a cigar and reading the sports page when I pushed open the heavy glass-fronted door. I breathed in a robust mingling of cigar smoke and bay rum. He looked at me over a curl of smoke, tugging at one long end of his mustache.

"I need a haircut," I said.

He heaved his heavy body out of the only barber's chair, chewed the end of his cigar, and scowled at my ratchety head. "Run over by a lawn mower, were you?" he said. I didn't reply, but climbed into the chair while he shook out a white cape, furling it across my front, securing it at the neck. He looked at me closely. "Aren't you one of them Kemp girls?"

"No."

He folded his arms, combing his mustache with his lower teeth. I glared at him and then softened. "It's all right," I said. "I'm allowed." I opened my hand and showed him two sweaty quarters. With a shrug, Vincent picked up his scissors.

The shock! At home, the shock of me with no hair (almost no hair – I still had hair on top), razored right up the back of my head, and my blatant disobedience caused Adele to take to her bed with a cold compress. My hair, or the lack of it, floored both Sylvia and Cynthia.

"Oh, golly!" Cynthia said. She blinked at me in awe. "Boy, that's really just . . . !" She tried to express her wonderment, but words failed her.

Sylvia said, "Well, I think it's disgusting. You look like a boy."

"Good," I said.

I stood outside Adele's closed bedroom door and at the top of my lungs explained: "I refuse to be a daughter and, from now on, I am your son. I refuse to turn into a disgusting, fat old woman and so I won't." And more quietly, my lips to the keyhole, I said, "I refuse to have a sixth sense, and from now on I don't because I am a son."

Marietta, who had just had two days off, leaned against the door frame of her own room across the hall. "No sense at all, I'd say," she muttered.

She wasn't supposed to have heard that last part, and I was crushed by her judgment. Unmasculine tears darted into my eyes.

Vanessa came out of her room, her left arm still in a cast and sling. Open-mouthed, she eyeballed me from the top of my boyish head to the toes of my scuffed boots. She pounded with her other fist on Adele's bedroom door. "Mother, you have to do something. If Ros is allowed to go around looking like a freak of nature, I'm going back to the city and never coming home again."

From deep within her room, her voice hollow, Adele issued directives: "Marietta, make a pot of tea. And I want each of you girls to take a cup quietly to your own room and remain there, without communicating for one hour. Then I will decide what's to be done."

Waiting for the tea to steep, Marietta looked critically at me. She made me turn in a complete circle to get the full effect. "Close, but no cigar," she commented. "You still have a girl's chin."

I walked briskly from the kitchen, refusing tea, of course. Adele had made the mistake of lumping me in with the girls. I sat alone in my room, trying to think everything through. I would not mention Lucy again, nor would Adele, I was quite sure. With her name banished, Lucy would disappear from the real world, wouldn't she? She would no longer haunt my dreams. On the issue of my metamorphosis into a boy, I held firm. My sisters could rant all they liked. Adele could have hysterics. I was no longer myself.

11

When I appeared downstairs wearing the same mud-colored breeches, the kneesocks unravelling near the top, and one of the rummage sale sweaters, which was roomy but quite handsome apart from the holes at the elbows, Adele was in the front hall on the phone. "Yes, thank you, Doctor." She heaved a weary sigh. "I suppose it's worth a try."

Glaring at me as she put the phone down, she said, "I lay the blame for this stupidity squarely on the shoulders of Lydia. Squarely. She should have refused to give you these ridiculous clothes. She should have prevented you from cutting your own hair in the first place." Adele looked not exactly broken as temporarily out of order.

Everyone gathered in the kitchen, where Adele was preparing dinner and Marietta watching through the window for her ride back to the city. I leaned against the door to the pantry, ready for an easy escape. Quietly, appalled, not looking at me, Cynthia said, "She can't really do that, can she? I mean, turn into –"

"Of course not!" Sylvia said. "Use your brain."

Marietta said, "You know, the mind is an amazing thing. People have been known to convince themselves into paralysis. Absolutely nothing physically wrong with them, and yet they collapse when they try to stand up."

"This is hardly the same thing, Marietta. And, don't put ideas into her head or we'll have her in a wheelchair next," said Adele.

Vanessa took up the topic. "If Ros goes around dressed like that, and with her hair all shaved up the back, people are going to call her names."

"Like what?" Cynthia wanted to know.

Vanessa glanced at Adele, who was frowning into her pile of sliced potatoes and onions. "A queer," she said, and watched her mother wince.

Marietta said, "Whatever the reason, it's Rosalind's choice to dress and look like a boy. Who wouldn't? No draggy skirts, no garters, no high-heeled shoes, no bras. Freedom, that's what she has, freedom."

"Freedom to look like a jackass," Vanessa said.

A car horn tooted outside and Marietta grabbed her suitcase, blew kisses, and was soon on her way back to Kingston to the hospital. I felt the loss of my only ally.

All through dinner my sisters eyed me when they thought I wasn't looking. Vanessa started in again, trying to make me see what an idiot I was. "You'll never get to wear lipstick, or have curls in your hair, or shop for a party dress. In fact, no one will invite you to a party. You'll never get asked to dance. You'll never have a boyfriend."

Cynthia stared at me, her fork halfway to her mouth. "You could ask a girl to dance," she said brightly.

"Cyn-thi-aw!" Sylvia said.

"Well, I just thought . . . it kind of makes sense."

"Could we please just drop this entire distasteful subject?" Adele said.

I spent a long time alone in my room that evening. Sitting on the side of my bed, I could just glimpse the top half of my head in the mirror above my dresser. I concentrated long and hard on that half-image until I began to relax. In the mirror, my forehead seemed broader, my features less delicate. I felt taller, stronger. I stood up and took long strides to the door.

Adele announced to her bridge club, and to the school, that I was going through a phase and had to be humored. Dr. Harmon had advised it as the best course of action for the moment. She said that Vanessa's fall had unhinged my mind.

Adele was enough of a warrior, though, to see the need for strategy during the trying times ahead. Yes, she would humor me, she told my sisters, up to a point. "I think we'll all be aware when we've reached it."

When I announced that, from now on, I would answer only to the name Ross, Adele sighed, "That's fine, dear."

I glanced up with suspicion.

On Monday, my first day at school as Ross, I clumped heavily down the hill, eyes trained on the sidewalk, on the cracks, on tufts of dandelion forcing their way between the cracks.

I entered the school yard through the boys' gate, mouth dry as chalk. I leaned against the fence, watching the game of scrub got up by the older boys and listened to them hollering at the little kids to get off the baseball field. At first, they didn't notice me. I took a breath and strode out onto the field.

Somebody called, "Hey, kid! Who asked ya? Get off, eh!"

"Who-zat?" somebody else asked.

"Some new kid."

It didn't take long for word to get around that Rosalind Kemp was pretending to be a boy. I felt an undertone of anger wherever I went. Most of the boys acted as though I didn't exist. They looked past me; jostled me clumsily with their shoulders; tripped over me with their big feet. They talked through my words, talked in front of me the way they would have behind my back.

The girls pretended not to see me at first. And then their eyes would pop wide and they tried to smother squeals of laughter behind inky hands. Carol Ann Hagen now sat behind me and took to ruffling my short hair. I squirmed out of reach, burying my head under my arms. When Miss Boyle was occupied at the blackboard, I turned around and whispered, "Quit it!" Carol Ann pouted and made little smacking kisses at me.

Miss Boyle kept me after school for a little talk.

"Why?" she asked simply. "Please just tell me why."

"It's a private reason," I said primly, trying to be respectful. I looked into Miss Boyle's eyes, hoping for a glimmer of acceptance, or even sympathy, but her eyes were busy darting from my fly-front to my shorn head and back again. She sent me to see the principal.

Mr. Pringle kept the infamous strap hung on a nail in his office. When discipline was needed, he meted it out, whack by stinging whack, usually to boys. Girls rarely got the strap. I sat on my slender hands on the edge of a chair inside the high-ceilinged office and wondered if this would be the end of my boyish self.

Mr. Pringle stood above me – a tired, sagging man smelling of chalk dust and well-worn leather shoes. He looked down wearily and shook his head, taking in my entire costume. "Thought I'd seen everything, but this beats all. Miss Boyle says you won't explain." Mr. Pringle fixed me with a beetle-browed scowl. Without turning his head, his eyes shifted threateningly in the direction of the strap and back to me.

"It's private," I murmured.

"Indeed. And I suppose you hear voices, telling you what to do."

I gave him a puzzled look. "No."

He went over to a bookshelf propped against one wall of his office, nodding his head. "Indeed," he muttered again. Grunting, he bent, extracted a book from a lower shelf, and returned, still nodding. He held out the book. "This is what happens to little girls who get ideas beyond themselves. Thinking they can be just like the boys."

I took the book. *Saint Joan,* it said.

"Open it."

Inside I saw that it was a play by someone named George Bernard Shaw.

"Joan got herself into a hot little mess, let me tell you. You read that, my girl, and write a book report on it and hand it in to me. You are to write out the lesson to be learned. Dismissed."

I hurried along the street, eyes down, *Saint Joan* stuffed into the book bag slung across my back. Girls glided past, giving me a wide berth. They tittered once they had passed and looked back for another shocking glimpse.

I took the usual route home, past the Presbyterian church, head down, thinking about reading the play. It wouldn't be so bad. I'd never read a play in a book – just mimeographed sheets. I could pretend to be all the characters at the same time.

Suddenly I was ambushed. Silent and fast, they rushed at me from the lane beside the church – Carol Ann and two other girls I hardly knew. I kicked as hard as I could and tried to twist away, but they dragged me into the shed behind the church, where people used to tie up their horses back in the horse-and-buggy days. The old horse manure still smelled. I know because they kept pushing my face into it.

"Good enough for ya, ya filth-pot!" one of the girls yelled. The girls were all yelling and panting and swearing.

This wasn't just kids ganging up. What I felt was hatred. Their eyes didn't even look human. It wasn't any of their business what I wore, or how short my hair was. This seemed like war, and somehow I was the enemy. I tried to ask what I'd done to them, but they twisted my arms and forced them up my back. I screamed because I couldn't help it. This made them laugh. They sat on my legs and ground my face into the cold muck.

"Y' morphradike!"

Carol Ann spit on me. She bounced on my legs and pulled my head up by the hair and squashed it down into the filth. When my nose started to bleed, they stopped. My forehead was bleeding and so was my mouth.

"Jeepers!" one of them said. "Lookit whatcha done!"

I closed my eyes.

"I never did it!"

"Get off her!"

They rolled me onto my back and I became a deadweight, my head lolling. I felt blood streaming from my nose across my cheek.

"Are you ever gonna get it, Carol Ann!" one of the girls taunted the leader of the pack.

"I didn't hardly touch her. Let's run!"

When their voices, hollow, echoing fear, drifted away, I sat up, tears streaming, hands raking muck from my face. I tried to be sick, but nothing came up. I checked my teeth, afraid they were falling out. I spat bloody guck out of my mouth. What if I had to get false ones like the old aunts? I limped home, my hand over my raw mouth, every part of me aching.

"My soul and body!" Adele was enraged when she saw me. "To think!" she said. "To just think that anyone would attack a child of mine!" She sputtered, gasped, took several deep breaths. She called Dr. Harmon. She called Chief Callan down at the police station, who was married to our second cousin. "The very idea!" she steamed.

"Who did this to you?" the constable who came to investigate asked me, but I said I couldn't remember. I didn't know what they might do if I told. The constable looked at my clothes. "You in some kind of costume pageant?"

"No," I said.

"Yes," said Adele.

He left without knowing quite why he'd been summoned.

Adele soon composed herself, tightening her lips, narrowing her gaze. As she marched me up to the bathroom to help clean me up, I noticed her pink cheeks. I saw a new light in her eyes. It was as if her bosom swelled and her shoulders broadened. She breathed heavily in and out, in and out. "My brood has been threatened!" she said.

As soon as she could, she phoned the principal and described what had befallen me. "I will speak to Miss Boyle," he said.

"And a mighty lot of good that will do," Adele said, as she hung up the phone.

I was allowed to stay home from school for a week, in lonely seclusion. Vanessa had gone back to her secretarial course. She had to work hard to catch up if she wanted to graduate with the other girls.

Adele went out a great deal – to do the shopping, to play bridge, to chair the Ladies Auxiliary, to organize hampers for the troops. At home she was busy sorting through outgrown clothing and putting it in boxes, trying new recipes, making lists for Edna, who worked for her three days a week. She scarcely saw me. When our eyes did meet, Adele gazed away in exasperation. Towards the end of the week, she said, "You've let me down, you know. You were such a pretty little girl."

After school, the twins avoided me and did their homework in their room. At the dinner table, they looked beside me or above my head. I felt formless – like something that could ooze out and run all over the floor. Rosalind had disappeared, but Ross had not yet solidified in her space. I was struggling through the play about Saint Joan. I now knew all about martyrs.

It took all my courage to go back to school, my face bruised and scratched. My attackers kept their heads down, still waiting for the ax to fall on their none-too-clean necks. It never did. I hadn't told on them. This, alone, gave me a sense of power, made me appreciate Joan of Arc. Whenever my attackers dared to look at me, I stared back, making my dark eyes as menacing as possible. But, I was lonelier than ever. Not even the nice kids would have anything to do with me. I knew what it was like to be invisible.

The boys called me dirty names that had to do with parts of my anatomy and laughed out loud in class. "Quiet, please, order in the classroom!" Miss Boyle would urge.

I couldn't risk using the boys' washroom, or even the girls'. Sometimes I had to sit still, legs tightly crossed, teeth clenched, and wait until I got home. Once I had taken a peek inside the boys' and been shocked by this trough kind of thing. It looked disgusting. And when I went into the girls', a lot of girls started screaming. When the final bell rang, I was the first one out.

The boys shot spitballs off the ends of their rulers when Miss Boyle's back was turned. They whizzed through the air and caught me on the cheek, on the neck. I learned to fire them back. From sheer tension, Miss Boyle broke her chalk three times. By the next week, Miss Boyle declared that she'd had about all she could take. She telephoned Adele, who agreed to attend a meeting in the classroom after school that would include me.

Adele arrived prepared for battle. She had carefully applied a flush of rouge to her handsome cheekbones. She had pulled tight the laces of her newest and strongest foundation garment. She wore a steely gray suit with imposing shoulder pads, and across these massive shoulders she had flung a fur neck-piece – the hide of a dead fox, its glassy eyes staring out behind.

Miss Boyle was, herself, a warrior to be reckoned with. She ushered Adele to a pupil's desk in the first row, beside me. She barricaded herself behind her own massive oak desk and began the battle. "Mrs. Kemp, this cannot go on. It is no longer a joke. It cannot be treated as a childish whim."

Adele drew a breath in order to retaliate, but very quickly Miss Boyle launched another offensive. "And furthermore, Mrs. Kemp, it distracts the other children." Miss Boyle's voice rang with confidence. She held the high ground here. She seemed to sense that Adele, for all her fox furs and her mighty bosom and her rouged cheeks, didn't have a leg to stand on. "I have a class of twenty-four pupils to teach," she said. "If they are busy laughing at your daughter, whispering amongst themselves about what she is allowed to wear to school each day, then I cannot teach them. I simply cannot."

I could see that Adele was seething. I wished she would look at the blackboard behind Miss Boyle, because even though Miss B. was enthroned behind her desk at the front of the classroom and looked as though she might win this battle, I had to smile. Someone had written something behind her. It was the start of a poem in her handwriting, but doctored after the dismissal bell by one of the kids in my class.

Bums

I think that I shall never see
A poem lovely as a bum.

I tried not to grin.

"Your daughter is a roadblock in the path of learning." Miss Boyle sat back in her chair, looking pleased with the picturesque way she'd said that.

I could see, though, that Adele was about to bring out her big guns. She cleared her throat. "Perhaps, Miss Boyle, you could begin by teaching your pupils the very rudiments of good manners. Teach them not to laugh at a person's clothing. Teach them not to whisper unkind things. I am alarmed that these lessons are not uppermost on the curriculum. Are your pupils allowed to laugh at fatherless urchins in rags? Do you not teach them to respect the costumes of other cultures? Do you allow them to attack and beat other children? Respect, Miss Boyle, and tolerance for those who look different! Dear me, I had no idea that education had reached such a pass. I shall certainly speak to someone about it. The superintendent of schools. The newspaper. The Home and School Association."

Miss Boyle looked taken aback, as if Adele might have a leg to stand on, after all.

"Thank you for your time, Miss Boyle. I have letters to write and telephone calls to make." Adele unfolded her armored frame from the confines of the desk and nodded in Miss Boyle's direction. Harry Warner, the superintendent, was Adele's first cousin by marriage; Morris Kendall, the editor and owner of the newspaper, was a family friend of long standing. And. The president of the Home and School Association was none other than her good self.

"Come along, Rosalind," she said.

Mesmerized by Adele's power, I grasped the sides of my desk, about to stand up. But suddenly remembering the point of this whole episode, I stayed where I was, running a hand self-consciously up the back of my close-clipped neck.

Glancing back, Adele closed her eyes briefly, took a deep breath, and said, "Come along, Ross – dear."

I tossed a honey-colored lock out of my eyes, tucked my baggy shirt down into the waist of Corny's best Eaton's catalogue trousers, and followed Adele as she marched out of the classroom without so much as a glance at Miss Boyle.

"It's perverted, that's what it is," I heard Miss Boyle say. Adele was halfway down the corridor. I glanced back in at Miss Boyle. She gave a little cough of disgust. A deposed queen. Behind her, the title of the revised poem stood above her hair like a crooked tiara.

Adele hurried away from the school and turned onto Church Street. I stretched my legs into a long boyish stride to keep up. Adele said, "This does not mean I condone it, you know. Not for one little minute. You *will* outgrow this."

I no longer needed to argue the point. I thought of myself as a boy, had made that decision about myself, and that's all there was to it. The rest of the family just had to accept it. The school had to accept it. That's the way it was with martyrs.

The fox's head glared glassily at me. I hurried ahead and opened the little gate that spanned our front walk, ushering my mother ahead of me.

*

As time passed, to avoid frustration, they began calling me Ross at home. I was deaf to any other name. At school I studied the way boys act, imitating their habits, kicking at stones, swearing. I put pennies in my pockets so that I could jingle them.

I handed in my book report on *Saint Joan* to Mr. Pringle. It had been a hard read, but I was able to make sense of it. It seemed to me that Mr. Pringle was actually on my side. I started the report by saying *Thank you for understanding how I feel. I have never read about Joan of Arc before. Now I can see how much we have in common. She had her reasons for turning into a boy and I have mine.* I described as much of the play as I could and ended by saying *The point of the story is that after they burn you in a fire until there is nothing left, everyone starts to feel sorry for you. Eventually they pass a law to say you are now a saint. This is almost like making you into a person again, but not quite. As a saint you will last forever, which would be quite nice if you were not already dead.*

He never even told me what he thought of it.

The superintendent of schools visited our class in person and apparently saw nothing disagreeable or unsightly in my clothes. He said something quietly to Miss Boyle and that seemed to be the end of it.

Of course, it wasn't. Miss Boyle went out of her way to make the class laugh at my expense. "Are you paying attention, *Mister* Kemp?" she would say, or, "Which of you boys left a jacket in the boys' washroom? Not you, I hope, Rosalind, I mean Ross." The class howled; they loved it.

My classmates continued to make my life miserable by tripping me, or bumping into me. "Oh, sorry," they'd say. "Didn't see you." I was invisible and so was everyone else. No one saw me and I looked no one in the eye.

One day, somebody pushed my face into the boys' drinking fountain. I cut my lip. After I got the blood to stop, I went up to my classroom. The class had already begun. While Miss Boyle gave a lecture on lateness and rudeness, I pulled all the stuff out of my desk and shoved it into my book bag.

"What are you doing?" Miss Boyle asked me.

"I'm quitting," I said. I heard a chorus of gasps.

"You can't quit. It's not allowed," Miss Boyle said.

I didn't say another word. I walked out of her class and out of the school.

Adele was at the kitchen sink peeling apples for a pie when I arrived home in the middle of the afternoon. "I quit school," I said.

She put down her paring knife, dried her hands, and turned, bracing herself against the sink. "Don't be foolish!"

My books clattered onto the kitchen table. I stood at attention, my shoulders hunched up almost to my ears. Adele folded her arms across her bosom. "You can just turn around and march straight back to school, young lady."

"I can't," I whispered.

"You can and will. Now."

"No."

A perilous silence. Adele looked as if she had not heard correctly, as if she could not believe that once again her will was being put to the challenge. "How dare you say no to your mother! March!"

I scarcely dared breathe. I stood, unblinking, locking eyes with Adele's.

"No," I said.

I saw panic in Adele's face; saw her press her fist into her chest, as if she felt too much blood rushing to her heart. She had always had control on her side. Now it had let her down.

In that moment, I knew something. My mother was only human. Adele blinked first, letting a heavy sigh escape. She turned, sagging, diminished, and plodded haltingly toward the stairs.

I was left slouching in my roomy shirt and Charlie Chaplin trousers, alone. Guilty. I fought back tears. *How had this come about?* I wanted to be victorious, but not at the price of seeing my invincible mother deflated.

I sat down at the kitchen table, a bully with a hat pin. *Step on a crack.* It was true. My mother's back was breakable. Tears darted into my eyes in spite of myself. The way Adele had challenged Miss Boyle and won had made me believe her immortal. But now I could see that she wasn't. She was growing old, and what did that mean? That I was growing up? Never. I shoved my hands into the depths of my pockets and jingled my two nickels and eight pennies.

The twins came home after school, aghast. More or less. They had heard the rumors, the smirking whispers from kids in my school that their little sister had quit. Sylvia said, "Goll!" Cynthia added, "It's just too . . . too. . . ."

Adele got out her notepaper. Within two days, Vanessa's reply lay open on the kitchen table. I saw my name (former name, actually) in it, so I read it. Her secretarial course finished, Vanessa had landed a job in a law firm. *It's exhilarating to be grown-up at last,* she wrote, *and involved with the real world. As for Rosalind, I'm sure she's just having a little nervous breakdown. She'll get over it.*

Adele saw me reading Vanessa's note. "She's probably right about you," she said. "Certainly nervous breakdowns are all you read about in the ladies magazines." Soon Beatrice wrote and tended to agree with Vanessa, apparently. As far as I knew, Marietta had not yet written back.

But I felt fine. No headaches, no stomachaches. I wasn't bursting into tears about nothing. I hadn't stopped eating the way nervous people were said to do. I was a normal boy.

"You will be taught at home," Adele declared that evening at dinner.

12

A dele put an advertisement in the paper requesting the services of a private tutor. Miss Sibyl Coombs, the only person to respond, arrived the following Monday. Leaning over the banister, I spied on her from the upstairs hall. She was bone-thin and wrinkled as a raisin. Her hollow cheeks, rouged to an orangey gloss, made her blue eyes look enormous – they seemed to roam everywhere, analyzing, memorizing. She looked as if she knew everything there was to know in the world. She kept her hat on, a funny turban affair that rose almost to a point. *Witch,* I thought. Or, no, *magician.* And then I thought *sorcerer* and stuck with that. She gave Adele her coat – a cape, really, with armholes. Adele ushered her into what had been Father's study.

I came quietly downstairs and stood outside in the hall near the open door, peeping in from time to time, hands deep in my pockets. I listened while Adele settled details of the arrangement.

She lowered her voice. "I should tell you, Rosalind is having a little trouble with her nerves. She's just at that upsetting age, you know."

"Puberty, you mean," Miss Coombs said boldly.

Adele cleared her throat and quietly agreed. "We feel that it's just a stage and so does the doctor." She went on, "For reasons I cannot begin to fathom, she's playing at being a boy. I know it's bizarre. It may even be unhealthy. But for the time being, for the sake of her delicately balanced mind, we've decided to humor her. She has never quite got over a bad accident that her sister had."

I made my boyish entrance at this point. Adele acknowledged me with a look of resignation. She introduced me to Miss Coombs as Ross.

Shyly, I came forward to shake hands, fingering the knot in my tie, conscious of my tight collar, of my slickly combed hair. Miss Coombs beamed her brilliant eyes at me. Adele, shaking her head, turned to leave. "Oh," said Miss Coombs, before she had quite left the room, "would it be too much trouble to ask you to bring a pot of tea? I find I'm much more lucid with a cup of tea at hand than without." Adele assured her it would be no trouble.

When she'd left, my tutor made a slight bow. "Allow me to compliment you on your choice of gender. I'd have done the same thing if I'd had the nerve. Girls' clothes were ridiculous in my day and still are, if you ask me."

"That's not why I did it," I said.

Miss Coombs waited for me to go on, and when I didn't,

she leafed unconcernedly through my schoolbooks, stacked on the desk.

Observing her, sizing her up – eyes, cheeks, hat, and all – I had a sudden desire to explain myself. Something about the brilliance of her eyes made me want her on my side, want her saying, "Yes, of course, I understand completely."

Presently Adele brought tea on a tray, along with her front-ranking china. When the door closed behind her, Miss Coombs pulled a small vial from her purse and poured a clear liquid from it into her cup. "I like my own sweetener," she explained, "my eau-de-vie." She drank deeply and her face creased into an elfin grin. "Now then, where were we? You dress as a boy to escape something." Her eyes were riveted on me.

"No. I do it to fool fate," I said suddenly, and before I knew it, I'd explained about having second sight, and about the whole seventh-daughter disaster. "Do you believe in second sight?" I asked. I think, in a way, I wanted her to say no. I wanted her to say that science has proved it doesn't exist.

Instead, Miss Coombs said, "Animals sense danger – why shouldn't people? Or," she said, after a pause, "consider this. Everything in the world has already happened and we come upon events by chance, some of us ahead of others. It's a possibility, and no sillier than a lot of other things we claim to believe. Or else this. There are things we simply know. There is a shared knowledge in the vastness of the world that some can more readily draw on than others."

I looked at my shoes.

"I see that you are sceptical. Well, well, so be it. But here is something you might take to heart. 'There are more things in heaven and earth, Horatio, than are dreamt of in your philosophy.' That is Prince Hamlet speaking. Shakespeare, you know."

I was silent. I hoped Adele wasn't listening on the other side of the door because, if she was, Miss Coombs would be out on her ear in two seconds flat.

Miss Coombs said airily, "My dream is to fly, to personally conquer gravity. Your dream is to conquer fate. Both are acts of hubris. Look it up."

I knew I was staring at her, knuckles pressed to my mouth, frowning with concentration.

"And, of course, what will we learn if we don't venture forth?" She made a helpless gesture with her hands, winked, and swallowed her tea. "Come. The observed world awaits. The realms beyond must unfold as they will." She drew a newspaper from her large briefcase. "Let us begin with the front page," she said. Rattling the newspaper into a convenient fold, she continued, "I met Mussolini years ago, before the present war, when I was last in Italy. He chews his food with his mouth open. A despicable man."

Miss Coombs and I read the headline news each day while she had her tea. I looked up words I didn't know, and drew maps of the enemy-occupied lands. Then we tackled the day's lesson. Whenever I glanced up, I would see her watching me over the rim of her teacup. Sometimes I drew caricatures of Hitler and Mussolini, Chamberlain and

Roosevelt and Prime Minister Mackenzie King. She looked critically at the drawings. "You have a gift," she said, "but it does not lie in the realm of spelling." She handed me back an essay with five spelling errors.

I rarely ventured beyond the front gate, now. My world consisted of the inside of our house, which was pretty big; the garden behind it; and the woods behind that. The private forest was my Eden. I guess, in a way, I was both Adam and Eve watching over ants, beetles, caterpillars, moles, chipmunks, squirrels, and raccoons, all dependent on the heels of bread I broke up and threw to them.

One day in late May, I suggested we have my lessons in the woods. Miss Coombs looked doubtful. "Please?" I wheedled.

After a swallow or two of tea, she nodded, shrugged, winked, and said, "Yes. Tomorrow we shall go outside. It will be an adventure."

It was sunny the next day, but with a cool breeze. She lugged along a book containing many colored reproductions of great works of art, the size and weight, almost, of a concrete slab. Gamely she followed me to the end of the garden and through the broken fence. She toted the book; I dragged two canvas chairs. We settled beside the natural pool, shaded by a young oak and a thick elm, its grizzled bark hoary with moss.

I soon became lost in the art book's reproductions: aged babies in the arms of unlikely Madonnas, rich golds, startling crimsons, a hook-nosed duke in profile, a pear-shaped wife-to-be promising herself with open palm to a pale husband. I asked questions, and Miss Coombs answered them at first, but, as the shadows lengthened and the cool breeze scattered last year's fallen leaves, she squinted in the dappled sunlight. Hunched like a bat in her chair, she wrapped her cloak more tightly around her, glancing over her shoulder, up into the trees, twisting her empty hands anxiously. We had come away without so much as a drop of tea.

"We must go back," she said. "We are not all suited to the enchantment of a forest."

"But it's early. We could move further around into the sun."

"Fleeting warmth," she said. She had a slight tremor, making her head nod in constant agreement. "A dying day. Leaves have fallen; they decay." She shivered. She seemed to be witnessing things I could not see.

She shrugged, but didn't wink. Her face was drawn, old; her eyes were without luster. In her cheeks, veins tinged the orange rouge, turning it puce. We gathered our belongings and hurried back along the path to the house. She glided ahead of me, her cloak rising and falling in the breeze.

"May I look at this book again?" I called.

"Yes," she said, over her shoulder, "but you will have to get the better of your own demons and visit me in my hermitage."

*

I was lonely. Marietta was taking some special medical course in Ottawa now and had very little time off. Vanessa was in love. In every letter home, she made some mention of a young lawyer who had recently been taken into the firm. Beatrice had her baby boy. Adele spent five days in Toronto with her, leaving me and the house in the care of the twins, who were now sixteen and doubly capable. I had just turned thirteen.

I worked hard until the day I felt sick. I tried willing myself not to be hot, but my skin felt raw and clammy. Miss Coombs left early and suggested to Adele that I be put right to bed.

I lay dreaming; dreamed, woke, and dreamed again. Shivering, I woke up, and when warmth returned, I threw off the covers and felt as if I were being burned alive. The heat spread painfully over every inch of my skin. Flames flared behind my eyelids. My throat caught fire. I could hear the roar of a blast furnace inside my ears.

Someone's hands rasped over my skin – my mother's, my sister Marietta's. "Don't touch me!" I tried to tell them, but my throat was too sore. They shifted and rearranged me, as if my arms and legs were sticks of kindling. When they placed cool damp towels on me, the fire smoldered. Sometimes I could hear what they said.

"Keep on with the same treatment, Del. That's all you can do at this point." The voice belonged to Dr. Harmon. Also the pipe smoke and the smell on his hands of something like Mercurochrome. I was trying to open my eyes to tell him how hot I was, but became sidetracked by dreams.

And then, a few minutes later, or days, the dreams faded, and my skin felt less scorched. Later still, I don't know how long, the dreams ceased altogether. Voices spoke real words.

I heard Dr. Harmon say, "Complete bed rest for a while yet."

I heard Adele say something about being over the worst of it.

"We don't want a relapse," Dr. Harmon said. "There's always that chance with scarlet fever. No point in rushing things. We'll keep an eye on her. Don't want a case of rheumatic fever on our hands, either, on top of everything else. This happens sometimes."

Adele said something, but I couldn't make it out.

"Ah, yes," the doctor said. After a pause, he went on, his voice so low I could scarcely hear. "Just keep on humoring her and I think you'll see her outgrow it. What is she – ten, eleven?"

"Thirteen," Adele said.

"Oh." Another pause. "She seems younger. Trifle small for her age." The doctor's voice was gravelly.

I squirmed under the covers, clasping my hands over my chest, and felt two mounds of flesh, which seemed to grow even as I listened. I tried to concentrate on my chest area, thinking *flat*, thinking *thin*. The mounds stayed precisely the same. I rolled onto my side. It meant nothing. I would concentrate harder in a day or two, when I felt stronger.

Although Adele and Dr. Harmon had moved closer to the door, I could still make out their voices. "She'll be starting to develop," the doctor said. "Sometimes after a severe illness like this, girls come along. Once she matures, she'll straighten around."

Adele wasn't given to sighs, but she heaved a mighty one now. "I sincerely hope so. I think I've just about had it with the child."

"You're a strong woman, Adele. You've managed this far. I'd be inclined to let her play out her charade a little longer, until we're past the dangerous stage. By summer you'll see a change, and she'll be back at school in the fall, raring to go."

"I wouldn't bet on it," I wanted to say.

The doctor was replying to something Adele had said about missing so much school. Miss Coombs, it seemed, was no longer available. She had gone south to look after her sister, who'd had a stroke. "Miss Coombs managed well in some areas," Adele said, "mostly, literature, history, and geography."

"Get her caught up in mathematics and science," Dr. Harmon said. "That's what she needs. And I know just the lad to help you out in that regard. He's got one degree, but intends to go back to university for another."

"A strange young man in the house, day in, day out?"

"Now, Adele, I've known him since he was a child. He lives with his mother, over in Oxford Landing. Father was a minister. Died some years ago. The lad's no threat. Come the summer, he'll be at loose ends, and could use the money. And he needs the challenge, for that matter. Tends to be a bit wrapped up in himself. Unusual lad."

"Unusual! Well, that's about the last thing we need around here. Just because I allow a certain level of . . . exotic behavior doesn't mean I run a home for the warped and undisciplined."

Dr. Harmon must have recognized a storm warning. He changed the subject. "Marietta still interning, is she? Must be nearly finished."

"She's taking some special course," Adele said, "and then what, I wonder? Lady doctors! Dear me."

"Oh, they're the coming thing. Excellent baby doctors."

"She'd be better to marry and have her own babies. Though what man would have her, I can't say, she's so headstrong."

"She'll find someone, I've no doubt. And the other girls?"

"We've had a letter from Vanessa. She's engaged to a man we've never even set eyes on. They want to be married in the fall, for heaven's sake. Couldn't even wait a year."

"Good for her. Married life will be the making of her. And with this war on, nobody waits very long to get married." He harrumphed, asked where he'd left his hat, and then returned to the earlier topic. "Well, if you do decide on a tutor, I think it would be in the child's best interests not to mention she's a girl pretending to be a boy. Bit too bizarre for a young man to adjust to."

"How young is he?"

"Oh, twentyish, I should think. At any rate, I'd let her be what she seems – a frail boy, just getting over a serious illness.

To do otherwise might prejudice the lad against taking the job at all."

The voices drifted away into the hall. I heard Adele say, "Perhaps I'll consider this young man, after all. Tell me more about him."

Getting better was dreamlike. I just had to lie there and let it happen. Vanessa came home, bringing her fiancé and her engagement ring with her. She brought both up to my room. I admired the ring and shook hands with Jack. He cracked jokes and made me laugh until my throat hurt, and Adele came in and said that that was enough excitement for one day.

When I was well enough, I sat propped up with pillows and looked at the book Miss Coombs had left as a parting gift. It was the book of portraits we had looked at together. On the flyleaf she had written *Joy, we are obliged to share. Grief, like physical pain, is a lonely state.*

"That's a bit morbid," Adele said, when she read it. "Why would she write that?"

I didn't know, but, somehow, I knew I would find out.

13

Summer weather came soon to Kempton Mills and Hill Street, and so, one Monday, from Oxford Landing, did the tutor.

The twins said that nobody at their school talked about me anymore. "All people yak about is the war and how badly it's going in France," said Sylvia.

"And Herb Morley," Cynthia added. "He's over there now. And that boy whose father works in the post office. They say he's missing."

"Oh, yes, and Faye Wirt's father. They had to let him go. It turns out it was a cat that was killed in the boxcar. Not Faye."

I was glad that I was no longer a topic of conversation, but sorry for the soldiers who were. I wasn't sorry for Mr. Wirt. A man who would murder a cat would stop at nothing. Faye Wirt could be anywhere.

Adele and Aunt Lydia continued to gossip over tea every Saturday. I overheard them talking about me. "It's her over-wrought imagination that's to blame," Adele said.

Lydia said, "One has to be so careful with children these days."

"Dr. Harmon says it won't last forever."

"Of course it won't."

"It's far better," Adele said, "to play along right now. If we forced her to conform, it could send her right over the edge."

"I will have a good talk with Corny about this. He'll understand," Aunt Lydia said.

As a gesture of goodwill, Adele had invited Corny to stay for the summer and share the tutor. Lydia was only too glad to take up the offer. She had often said, "If only that boy would apply himself, he would be at the top of the class. He'll never get ahead in this world if he doesn't." Readily, Lydia agreed to share the cost. Adele was pleased with the bargain.

Marietta was home for the summer, doing a locum, as she called it, assisting the older doctors. "It's perfect," she told Adele. "It's a chance to show these folks who believe women doctors are less competent than men the error of their thinking."

"Quite right," Adele said. I saw her cheeks redden slightly.

"Not only that, it gives me time to decide what I want to do with my life as an M.D."

In a deck chair behind the house, I toasted myself in the bone-warming sun. The scent of orange blossom drugged the June air. A breeze tossed my hair, newly trimmed by Cynthia. I let my eyes rest on cloud puffs as they bundled past, knowing I was safe. I saw only clouds without shape, without pattern, without portent. I rolled up my sleeves to the elbow to tan my arms, and leaned my head back against the striped canvas. Scarlet fever had left me feeling languid and ghostly. I heard the *thrum* and *purr* of an engine. Corny banged through the screen door and clattered down the back porch steps.

"He's here! He has a motorcycle!" Corny's voice still searched the airwaves for a suitable range. It wavered between a shortwave screech and static. He could still split eardrums.

"Corny!" I got his attention with a rival screech that hurt my throat. "Don't forget!"

"Huh?"

I had to whisper. "I am Ross. Always have been. Always will be."

"I know, I know." He started toward the approaching vehicle in the driveway.

"Don't spill the beans about me to the tutor."

"Why would I?"

"You might forget; you might let Ros slip out."

Corny turned and examined my face for a moment, his own a puzzled frown. "I just don't get it. Aren't you a little too old to be this weird? People think you're off your rocker. My mother said so."

"Is that what you think, too?" I looked seriously into Corny's eyes, forcing him to look back into mine.

His frown softened. He didn't know whether to look at my eyes or my mouth. A sigh escaped. "No, that's not what

I think. You can be the queen of Sheba and it's still all right with me," he said. "Or the king of Siam."

The motorcycle putted to the end of the driveway in the backyard. The engine sputtered and died. Corny and I watched a young man remove a leather helmet and hang it on the handlebar. Still astride, he ran a hand through his hair and nodded in our direction.

Marietta came out onto the back porch to meet him. She was in charge for the time being. Adele had taken the train to Toronto to be with Beatrice and the baby while her husband, Dalton, was away taking a course. The twins managed the house and Marietta kept a sharp eye on me.

The tutor swung off the motorcycle, leaned it against the garage, and walked toward us. He limped! His left foot was raised slightly at the heel, and turned in. We all stared.

Marietta came first to her senses and went to him with an outstretched hand, smiling a welcome. "Hello, Mr. Hope." She made the introductions. His name was Adrian, he said, and asked us to call him by his first name. He smiled brightly at Marietta.

Corny and I were both a little tongue-tied. Adrian smiled at us. "Shall we get started?" he asked. He limped back to his motorcycle and took books from the saddlebags. Marietta said she'd leave us to it and hurried inside to get ready for her day.

Corny and I locked eyes and grinned. "He's nice, isn't he?" Corny whispered.

"Is he ever!"

We set up school at the end of the garden in the shade of the encroaching thicket, using a bridge table and folding chairs. On rainy days we stayed inside, seated around the dining room table. Marietta always had a cup of coffee ready for Adrian when he arrived early each morning, and usually sat with him for a few moments before leaving for the hospital. They had friends in common at university and discovered much to talk about.

Adrian Hope was calm and quiet. I liked the way his dark hair fell over his brow and he had to toss it back. I studied each of his features in detail and in the evenings, in my own room, I drew them. *Eyes of a poet,* I thought, *head of an emperor, shoulders of a Greek god.* Adrian's one flaw was his limp.

He was eager to have Corny and me learn. If we failed to master something, he seemed to take it personally. He would pull at his chin, his forehead creased, his eyes downcast. I drilled Corny in the evenings, just to prevent Adrian from getting discouraged. When we were able to divide fractions without a mistake, he smiled as if it was the most important moment of his life.

I began to find the weekends long. Sometimes Corny went home to help his father with the farm, returning Sunday night, eager for the new week to begin. We spent Sunday night talking about Adrian, remembering things he'd said the week before, and making up stories about why he limped. "You two have Adrian on the brain," Marietta said.

As July drifted along, I became restless. I paced the house in the evening, sitting down only to get up again. "Light somewhere, for heaven's sake," Marietta said.

In the early morning before class, I prowled the dew-damp garden, round and round its perimeter. I was beginning to feel caged, not safe. In the bathroom mirror, I saw only eyes and cheekbones. The rest of me didn't seem to be there.

Except during school hours. Adrian gave my life shape. He looked at us both so earnestly when he was explaining something that I was jealous. I wanted him to look only at me. I wanted to be the teacher's pet. I memorized the way he compensated for his limp. His curious limp. I wanted to believe it had something to do with an evil magician. I worked so hard for him that mathematical equations began to spill into my dreams.

As for Corny, I could tell by the way he looked and talked that he was prepared to fall down and worship our tutor, as well as the tutor's motorcycle.

Each day began like the last. In the distance, the whine of Adrian's motorcycle, a roar at the corner, a puttering up the drive, a final sputter. Smell of exhaust. Corny was always right there to greet him and wheel the machine over to lean against the garage. Marietta would come outside and say, "Isn't it a glorious morning?" Together they would sit on the back porch steps and drink coffee, shoulder to shoulder. Marietta would say something and Adrian would turn to look at her. I watched them laugh together. I saw Adrian sigh, get up slowly, make Marietta a half-salute, and turn toward Corny and me at our makeshift desk.

Sometimes I leaned on my elbow while Adrian was directing his attention to Corny, pencil working, my notebook shielded from view. I would concentrate on the line of Adrian's jaw, the set of his neat ears. A few more quick strokes. If Adrian happened to look up, I turned the page and sat with hands folded.

"Morning, boys," he greeted. "You're looking chipper." In the dewy morning, scented with freshly mown grass, he sat down at the table at the end of the garden and gave us both a friendly smile. I wondered what Adrian thought of me. I sometimes saw him glance at my fair hair, scattered around my head like a shiny bowl. "Turn to your science notebooks," Adrian said.

At about midmorning, I was aware of Adrian sitting back, observing me and Corny, watching Corny squint at the science problem as if that would help him concentrate while his tongue explored the inside of his cheek. I felt his glance as I puzzled out the speed of falling bodies, raking a sweaty hand through my hair, pushing it into haystacks, creating a doodle in the corner of my book – stars, a moon, heavenly bodies falling through space. A little picture of Adrian.

*

One rainy day, Adrian came quietly into the dining room after his coffee with Marietta and glimpsed a drawing getting some finishing touches. I quickly covered it, and flushed deeply. Adrian must have recognized himself because he looked uncomfortable. He cleared his throat. "You seem to have a talent for drawing. May I have a look at it?"

I handed it over and got up abruptly to look through the dining room window at rain pelting the hollyhocks at the side of the house. I kept my back to Adrian, hands in my pockets.

"This is really good." He sounded a little surprised. "Have you had lessons, or did you just pick it up?"

"Picked it up."

Corny bounded down the stairs, ricocheting off the newel post and through the dining room door. His homework flew out of his grasp and we all bent to pick up the pages, the drawing forgotten. Before long, we were hard at work.

Soon we had a stretch of sunny days, and decided to start earlier and finish earlier because of the heat. At the end of one sweltering day in August, we lolled on the grass in the shade. Corny asked Adrian if he had a girlfriend.

"Corny-y-y! What a thing to ask!" But I looked earnestly into Adrian's face, anxious for his reply.

He scowled into the haze and back at us. "Top secret information," he said.

"*Aw*, come on," Corny insisted. "Give. We won't let on we know."

It was too hot to work. Adrian played along, cautiously though, as if the situation could get out of hand. "You go first," he said to Corny. "Who's your one and only? Tell us her name."

"Oh, *jeez*," Corny said, looking embarrassed. His eyes slid toward me and quickly away. "I don't really have one, I guess. You do, though. You must."

"Are you kidding?" Adrian laughed. "Who'd want an old stumblebum like me? Girls want someone they can dance with. 'Fraid I'm not in the running. So to speak. How about you, Ross? Who's your girlfriend?"

I had been waiting for the question and had already begun to flush. By the time Adrian looked at me, I knew I was scarlet. "Don't be idiotic. I'm too young," I snapped.

Adrian looked at Corny and shrugged. Corny snorted with laughter so hard that he nearly fell off the folding chair.

"Corny!" I made my eyes murderous.

Sometimes, after lessons, we walked in the woods, where it was cooler. We had to beg Adrian to go with us at first. Embarrassed, he muttered, "I wouldn't be able to keep up."

I took his wrist and pulled him gently through the opening in the fence. "It's not a race," I said. I put my hands in my pockets and followed the path we'd worn down as small children, walking with the swaying swagger I'd picked up from Corny. I thought I caught sight of something shiny, blue-specked, in the hole of a tree, but turned away. It was nothing.

I whistled through my teeth, ambling, glancing shallowly right, left, straight ahead. The only things to observe were surfaces, gray rocks, gray tree trunks, sometimes a gray squirrel.

Corny said, "Why can't we have our lessons beside the pond?"

Adrian smiled. "It's tempting. Like something out of Rousseau's *Emile*. But, no, you wouldn't concentrate on your work."

"Sure we would."

I thought about Miss Coombs and her uneasiness about being so far away from her tea, with its comforting eau-de-vie.

Adrian said, "Better stick with tables and chairs, I guess. I have to earn my pay, after all." I know he was thinking about Adele. In a businesslike interview while she was home from Beatrice's for a few days, she had quizzed him about his knowledge of science and mathematics.

"Is this your field?" she had asked.

"No," he said, "but I know I can teach them at this level." He started to go over his curriculum, opening one of his books for her, but Adele stopped him. "It makes me dizzy just looking at the diagrams. Straight lines," she said. "Teach them everything you can about lines and squares and solving problems. That's what life is about."

But, one hot day, he brought along the book titled *Emile*. He opened it near the pond. "My grandfather gave me this when I entered university," he said. "It meant a lot to me because I always thought he hated books. He can't read English."

"That must be boring for him," I said.

"He gets a German magazine in the mail once a month, or used to. It's stopped coming. Held up at customs, they told him at the post office. 'We're not letting any subversive Kraut literature into the country' is actually what they said to him."

"Is that true?" I asked.

"Course it's true," Corny said. "And bloody right, too."

Adrian shrugged. "My grandfather's pretty harmless. It was just a farming magazine. He had a farm in Western Ontario before he came to live with us, after my father died."

"My father died, too," I said.

Adrian nodded at me sympathetically. Corny looked left out, with both parents alive and kicking. "So where do you live?" Corny broke in.

He told us about Oxford Landing, a quiet village not far from Kempton Mills. I loved watching him as he talked, and kept thinking up more and more questions. Both Adrian and Corny had unbuttoned their shirts in the sweltering heat.

"No more questions," he said, finally. He picked up his book and began to read aloud from *Emile*, which was really boring but we encouraged him to keep going. Both Adrian and Corny were stripped to the waist, now. Corny's shoulders were freckled, as well as his scrawny chest. He took off his shoes and socks, rolled up his pant legs, and stood in the shallows of the pond.

I sat a little apart, leaning against a tree, my shirt buttoned to the neck, wishing I had my drawing book. Adrian had the body of a grown man. A little dark hair on his chest. More under his arms. Under Corny's arms, too.

"Let's go swimming," said Corny.

Adrian tucked his foot back protectively and circled his knees with his arms. He shook his head. "You two go if you want."

I glared at Corny, who was now aware of his mistake. *"Nah,"* he said. "Some other time."

Corny's interest in the motorcycle was unflagging. At the end of each day, he walked with Adrian to watch him get on, start it, rev the engine. Every day he had a comment. "That's a darn fine machine" was his usual opener. Adrian always agreed.

"Hard to operate?" he finally asked, with a look of longing on his face.

"No, not really." Adrian could be maddeningly dense. He started the thing and putted down the driveway with a wave of his hand.

At last Corny reached the end of his patience. One day he said straight out, "Bet I could drive that baby." His voice vibrated with hopefulness. Once he seized an idea, it stuck. "Come on," he begged, "give me a driving lesson."

I squeezed in between the two, interested, envious. I got in front of Corny to examine the starter, the gears, the fuel tank. "You're in my way," Corny said, and jostled me aside so he could stand next to Adrian. "So, how do you change gears? Let me take it to the end of the driveway."

I slumped against the garage, watching Adrian limp after Corny as he drove slowly down the driveway. Adrian was shouting directions over the sputtering engine. Corny and Adrian. Adrian and Corny. "Let me try it again," Corny yelled.

Adrian looked over his shoulder at me sitting hunched, disappointed. He took his machine back from Corny, who gave it up with a comradely backslap. I wished Corny would suddenly get scarlet fever. Or take rat poison.

"Hop on," Adrian said to me. "You'll have to be content to be a passenger until you muscle out a bit." I got on awkwardly and found a place for my feet. "Hang on," he said.

I hung on to Adrian's belt as we put-putted down the driveway. I grasped the sides of his shirt as we turned onto the road. We roared along Hill Street, past neighboring houses, the town spread out dizzyingly below. I put my arms around Adrian's body as Hill Street became a dirt road. We roared along it raising dust, giving cows behind a fence something besides their cud to think about. I pressed my face into Adrian's back and breathed in the scent of soap and starch and tangy summer sweat. I was lightheaded. At a tee junction, Adrian slowed and came to a halt. I didn't want to release him, but I had to sit back. Adrian supported the cycle with his good foot. "Are you all right?" he asked, turning to look.

"Mm-hmm!" I said nodding, eyes wide, trying to look unmoved. I could barely speak, remembering the shape of Adrian's back and the ripple of muscles over his ribs.

"Thought you were scared, the way you were hanging on."

"*Mm-mm.*" I shook my head. I could see where Adrian's beard would have been if he hadn't shaved. Our eyes met. Adrian's were gray-green and made me think of a picture I'd seen of a storm at sea. I saw Adrian's puzzled expression before he turned away, as though he sensed something unreal in the situation.

Adrian made a wide arc and we headed back. Pressed against him once again, I had a tremendous urge to crush my mouth against his back. What if Adrian could feel my bound breasts? I almost wished he could. I turned my head. My lips lightly brushed his shirt.

Adrian brought the machine to a stop in front of our house near the gate. I clambered off and stood on the road close to him. "I've got to go, now," Adrian said quickly, roughly, I thought.

I nodded, looking up at him unsmiling, hands in my pockets, shoulders hunched. His hair was all blown about and he ran a hand through it. I couldn't stop myself looking at him.

Frowning, Adrian turned away and said, "Go as far as page twenty-five in the brown book. And do the next five problems. We've a lot of ground to cover to get you caught up. And give Corny a push," he added, revving the machine, eager to hit the open road. "He needs to work harder." He seemed to lose his balance for a moment as he started off. He drove slowly, as if he could not quite trust the slant of the road.

I went up to my room, my knees wobbly as I climbed the stairs, and lay on my bed.

Corny thumped up after me and barged in. "What's the matter with you?"

"Nothing."

"Well, listen," he said, "stop butting in on Adrian and me. You're always trying to hog him."

I didn't answer. I was reliving the experience of Adrian's body against my own.

"Are you sick?"

"Yes."

Corny stood over me, looking frightened now.

I closed my eyes like a corpse while a delicious shiver trembled through my entire body.

Corny ran to find my sisters.

14

Sylvia came running with a thermometer. My temperature was normal, but she told me to stay in bed until Marietta had a look. When Marietta came home, she rushed upstairs to put a cool hand on my forehead. "What's wrong?" she asked. "Did something happen to you? You look as though you've had a shock. Corny said you had a ride on Adrian's motorcycle. Obviously it was too much excitement."

All night I lay wakeful, aching inside, wanting something I wasn't able to describe. In the morning I was torn between staying in bed, half-sick, but parted from Adrian; or being at his side, suffering, knowing he would never feel for my boyish self what I felt for him. In the end, I dragged myself out of my clammy bed. Better to suffer at his side than from such a distance.

"Back to bed!" Marietta ordered, feeling my forehead with the back of her fingers. "We're not taking any chances."

"I'm fine." My voice sounded strained and I knew my eyes were too bright.

Marietta was insistent. She fixed me with a firm scowl, giving orders to the twins to tie me down if necessary and to phone Mother only as a last resort. "If you have no temperature by late afternoon, you can get up. Drink some ginger ale."

"You're not my boss."

"Oh, yes I am," Marietta said, on her way out the door. "I'll phone at noon."

I heard Adrian's motorcycle and got up to look through my open bedroom window. Corny, on hand as usual, relieved Adrian of his machine. Marietta came out. I could barely hear what she was saying, but caught enough to know that it was about me and my supposed illness. Adrian nodded sympathetically. I saw Marietta looking up at him, saying something about her work at the hospital. I felt a pang of jealousy when he patted her arm. He turned then, and limped off with Corny toward the end of the garden. I saw Marietta standing quite still in the driveway, watching him go. I saw her gently finger the arm Adrian had touched.

I went back to bed and lay there daydreaming all morning. There was a closeness in the air that could only be dispelled by rain. I was hot, but not because of fever. I knew all about fevers and this was different. It involved excitement and yearning. My skin tingled, needing to be touched, soothed.

The twins brought me lunch and took my temperature, debating over the position of the mercury, but agreeing, finally, that it was normal, or maybe a tad below normal. They told me to stay in bed.

When they returned downstairs, I got dressed. I went outside while Sylvia and Cynthia, oblivious to all but the household chores, wrestled with a sheet caught in the wringer of the washing machine.

Adrian and Corny were not in the backyard, so I assumed they were at the pond. I met them near the Elephant tree, returning through the sultry atmosphere. "It's quitting time," Adrian said. His voice was music to me, a full orchestra, although he spared me scarcely a glance.

"He's letting me take the motorcycle on the road!" Corny informed, at high volume.

Adrian kept walking. "Come on, let's get going." He didn't ask me how I was; he didn't even look at me. I felt slapped.

Stunned into action, I caught up and said, "What about my schoolwork? Don't you care about me?"

Adrian paused, looking trapped. He told Corny to go ahead and check the gas level. For a moment he studied me, concern on his face. He said in a kind voice, "Sorry, Ross. You look a bit washed-out. Marietta said you're still getting over scarlet fever."

I looked down at my feet, afraid of tears coming into my eyes. "I'm all right now."

"Glad to hear it. Mind if I give you some advice?" He cleared his throat, stammering, stumbling over his words. "I . . . you know. . . ." He began again. "You . . . you should really try and toughen up a little, you know?" I felt my cheeks flush red-hot. "Do you know what I mean? You don't want people to think you're a bit of a Nancy, do you?"

"Hey, Adrian!" Corny was coming back.

Head down still, I kicked up hunks of grass with the toe of my boot.

Adrian's voice became gruffer as Corny approached, "Try your best. For now, go on back to bed till your sister comes home. She'll get you straightened around."

I was burning with shame. What a confusing mess! I wanted to hate Adrian. I looked for something to throw at his back as he limped along, shoulder to shoulder with Corny. Instead, I dragged behind, tears blinding me. I noticed that Corny was walking with a hint of a limp, too.

Corny turned. "You heard Adrian," he said smugly. "Go on inside." He finally had Adrian all to himself. His big chance to hang around with the men. Corny's limp switched sides, but was more apparent.

I stopped following them. Adrian turned and said, not unkindly, "You'll feel better tomorrow. Go on."

The two, man and boy, busied themselves with the motorcycle. The engine came to life. Adrian got on behind, and I listened to it *put-put* down the driveway. I would not go inside. I made my way once again toward the gap in the fence, dragging the back of my fingers across my wet cheeks, sniffing hard. I could hear the motorcycle roar along the street beside the woods, and tried to block out the sound as I ran, stumbling now and then over tree roots, toward the pond.

At the water's edge, I sat on the grass and swatted mosquitoes, damning Adrian, blasting the heat, cursing what had pushed me into this bizarre disguise. I took off my boots and socks and rolled up my pant legs, exposing down-covered shins. The fair hairs darkened underwater. I rolled up my sleeves and undid the top buttons of my shirt. Rank waftings from my armpits made me wrinkle my nose. I tried washing the odor away with handfuls of water, but now my shirt was dripping wet. I took it off and spread it on the grass. In my tight under vest I leaned back on my elbows, looking up at the sky, gray and threatening above the trees.

Beatrice and her husband, Dalton, crept into mind. I tried to imagine my sister aching over Dalton. I remembered the way Marietta had looked at Adrian that morning and felt defeated.

It was unbearably hot. Thunder groaned in the distance. I undid my belt and the buttons of my trousers and squirmed out of them, and out of my underpants. The parched grass beside the pond was uncomfortable on my bare bottom. I stood, rolled up my vest, and yanked it over my head. Spreading out my clothes for easy access, I spotted Adrian's book, *Emile*, left behind, partly hidden in the long grass. I picked it up. *Adrian R. Hope* was written on the flyleaf. I brought it to my lips. *Queen's University*, I read then, *111 Lower Union Street, Kingston*. I caressed the book against my naked breasts and felt a longing.

And then felt silly. I could imagine Adele saying, " *Tch!* The very idea!"

Guiltily, I put the book back down in the grass. Some-where in the distance, the motorcycle buzzed the dense air.

I stepped onto the submerged rocks at the edge of the pond and plunged in. The icy water, its source an under-ground spring, shocked me. I took in mouthfuls and drooled it out, ducked my head under, shook water out of my eyes and ears like a dog. I crept out onto the rocks and then flung myself back into the pond. The rain started. I turned my face up to be slapped by rain splats, drinking them.

I was soon cold and climbed out, finding the rain warmer than the pond. Standing in the tough grass, I wel-comed the stinging rain with open arms and closed eyes. I began thinking about how wet my clothes were getting. *And Adrian's book!*

I opened my eyes and there was the book's owner in person. I froze.

Adrian gaped at me through the underbrush like some pop-eyed explorer, stout Cortez, deceived by the natives, shocked, mortified. "I . . . I . . . I," he said. He backed away a step, nearly tripping, aghast, face ashen. Rain running down his cheeks. Stalled, seized by sudden paralysis. Both of us, captives of the moment.

I dropped to the ground, trying to disappear. *Shouldn't one of us say something?*

"My . . . my . . . my . . . book!" His mouth was a black *O.*

Wildly, I thought of trying to explain. *Oh, Lord! And say what?* The mad twin sister, recently escaped from the attic. I wound myself in the scant covering of my arms as insane laughter boiled up and snorted out into the rain-drenched silence.

His face was scarlet, disbelieving.

I felt I would froth hilariously forever, mad as a dog. A maniac! I heaved myself toward my clothes, tripping, falling on them. Crippled by laughter, I stuffed my shirt into my mouth. I couldn't stop. Crying, now, great gulps.

I grabbed at my sodden clothes but couldn't get into them, struggling, choking out impossible tear-drenched laughter.

Adrian was gone.

I caught my breath in little gasps, little sobs. I punched fists through the sticking shirtsleeves, got the shirt wrapped around me, tied the tails in a knot. Got the trousers pulled up, managed one button and the belt. I was shaken, off and on, by ripples of silent laughter. I stuffed my underpants into my pocket, noticing a dark stain, wondering. I rescued *Emile* and poured rainwater from the dish of its warping cover.

I left my boots and socks behind. Corny's. Too big, anyway. I picked my way on tender feet as carefully as I could through the teeming woods, bent over, insides seizing up. At the gap in the fence, a sharp rock grazed the side of my foot as I caught sight of Marietta home from work, dashing to get out of the rain. I opened my mouth and wailed her name.

Howling, struggling through the broken fence, I felt Marietta's arm around me, supporting me. Something warm running down the inside of my leg. *Dear God,* I thought, *what now?*

Marietta led me inside. Warm, dry, comforted, I accepted her observation that I was a woman, now. She explained in more detail than Adele had, gave me supplies, told me how to deal with it. Corny tried to barge into my room, but Marietta made him buzz off. In the evening, Sylvia and Cynthia escaped to the movies, and Marietta phoned Adele, who thought she should come home. "No need," Marietta said. "Not the end of the world. She'll cope. We all do."

Snuggled into the deep couch in the sitting room and bundled in pajamas and an old flannel hand-me-down bathrobe, I hid behind the newspaper, halfheartedly reading about the war. I listened with one ear to Marietta. I could hear Adele quacking through the phone. Marietta murmured, "We'll see. Lots of things around here to fit her. Or, we could go shopping." I was too tired to care what role I would play tomorrow.

I was aware of Corny lounging at the other end of the couch, his feet on the ottoman, pretending to concentrate on Eaton's catalogue. I caught him looking at me from time to time, but his eyes quickly returned to the page in front of him. I wondered briefly what section he was studying. I had happened upon him one day taking great interest in a page devoted to brassieres, and he'd turned pink. This afternoon, Marietta had explained the facts of life to him. I knew because I listened at the door of his room, formerly Vanessa's. I heard him say, "Shut up. I hate that kind of stuff. Anyway, I already know about it."

Unable to resist, I peered around the door. "Liar!"

He glared, blame in his eyes, as if I'd wrecked everything, desecrated his fairy tale. No longer a mermaid, I had legs – hairy ones – and great smelly feet.

Sitting with the catalogue on his lap, Corny took a deep satisfied breath and let it out. I could tell how much he liked himself. No hidden wells, no leaks. Seamless. He was masculine. Perfect. He turned toward me, briefly, and I saw pity cross his face. He gave his attention to the catalogue again, flipping over to men's work boots.

I went to bed, exhausted.

The phone rang. I could hear Marietta's voice. In a few minutes, she called up the stairs, "No lessons for a few days. Adrian's come down with something."

After a careful moment, I asked tensely, "Did he say anything about me?"

Marietta said, "No. Why? Did you make him sick?"

I didn't answer.

A week passed with no news from Adrian. Marietta said she hoped he was all right. We tried to telephone his home in Oxford Landing, but the operator said they didn't have a phone. They used a neighbor's when they had to make a phone call.

"How would she know?" I asked.

"Operators know everything," Marietta said. "Like God."

I still adored Adrian, but at the same time detested him. He had seen me in the raw. Heard my crazed laughter! If I saw him again, I might suffer another attack.

I wore the new undergarments Marietta bought for me and the new short-sleeved blouses, but I refused to part with the fly-fronted trousers. I walked around with my hands in my pockets and my shoulders hunched together, trying to keep from flying apart, or leaking away to nothing.

Summer was slipping toward September, with no further word from Adrian. I could stand it no longer. I had to see him, to explain, or at least leave a message for him. Early one sunny afternoon, I took my bicycle from the garage, put some drawing materials into the basket, and told my sisters I was going sketching.

It took almost two hours to get to Oxford Landing. The road into the village ran downhill, toward a shaded bend. Set well back beneath massive elms, a gabled house seemed to pass judgment on comings and goings along the main street. On this hazy August afternoon, I provided the only coming, and soon, I felt, would also provide the only going. The windows glinted, making me wonder if I was observed. Beside the house was a church. I came upon more houses and then a store boasting a post office. I would ask where Adrian Hope lived.

I wheeled my bicycle up to the store, leaned it against a telegraph pole, and went in. It was like the inside of a tree, all dark wooden counters and shelves. A man behind the counter examined me briefly over his shoulder, and turned back to his task of hooking something down from a high shelf with a pole. A customer, a woman, her flower-decked hat skewered to her head with a hat pin, rested one hip on a high stool near the counter. She looked up from her shopping list to study me, obviously not liking what she saw. She took in my short hair, flying every which way, my print blouse, and the trousers. She looked at the storekeeper with a lift of her eyebrows.

"Can I help you?" he asked.

"*Um*, I wondered where, *um*. . . ." *What if the woman was Adrian's mother?* I'd die. "I guess, probably, not." I hurried out into the blue haze.

Starting down the road on my bicycle, I wobbled before getting it going right. When I looked up, Adrian, unsmiling, was standing beside the road in front of the gabled house, watching me.

The very sight of him took my breath away. I put my foot down to steady the bike, hopping on one foot to stop it. The bike slipped from my sweaty grasp and fell over. If he didn't think I was an idiot before, he would now. Pastels burst from their box and went flying. Art paper scattered in the dust.

Adrian helped me collect my things, carefully avoiding my eyes. If our hands actually touched, it would be like an electric charge.

A sealed envelope with his name on it lay on the road between us. "That's for you," I said. I concentrated on blowing dust from my art pad, brushing at it, smudging, grinding the dust in.

He picked up the envelope.

"Read it," I said. I had written *Dear Adrian,* but had wanted to say, "My dearest Adrian." *I am sorry I laughed. I did not mean to. I wasn't myself.* (This last bit was scribbled out because the idiotic truth of it had affected me all over again, had made me writhe with helpless hysterical laughter.) *You may think we are all odd pretending I was a boy, but there is a good reason for it. Which maybe I can tell you sometime, but not right now. Just trust me that the reason is good. We want you to come back. We need you.* (Safety in numbers.) *I will not embarrass you ever again.* I had debated about the ending, but wrote, finally, breathlessly, *Your loving pupil, Rosalind.* I added a postscript. *You don't have to call me Ross any longer.*

He took a long time to read it, and when he finished, took a deep breath, looking me right in the eye. I couldn't look away. He wasn't smiling.

"Don't be angry," I said.

"What should I be? You've been playing a joke on me."

"It wasn't a joke. It's the farthest thing from a joke."

"Why did you do it?"

"I was hot. I wanted to go for a swim."

He interrupted, impatient. "Why," he repeated, teeth clenched, "why pretend to be a boy?" He looked away.

Should I try to explain?

The woman from the store walked toward us, her crocheted shopping bag bulging at odd angles. Her eyes signaled disapproval. Adrian nodded, unsmiling. She nodded, lips too tightly pursed to smile. "Furinners!" we heard her mutter.

"Could we sit somewhere?" I asked. "In the shade?"

On the lawn beside the gabled house, we sat in two armchairs made from split cedar logs. My bicycle lay in the grass. Adrian had brought us out glasses of iced tea. I was ready to explain. "Sometimes I can see that something is going to happen," I blurted.

He waited.

"I mean, sometimes bits and pieces, shapes, form a pattern and I find myself staring at the pattern. Right into it. And sometimes it reveals something – things I don't want to know. A disaster. But not always. Sometimes it's money. Or a fall from a tree, or a . . . a missing person. . . ." I glanced at him as he stared back.

"Like a clairvoyant?"

"Sort of."

There was a long ruminating pause. He cleared his throat. "It's a bit of hocus-pocus, isn't it?"

"Maybe," I said, hopefully.

"But I still don't understand why you would pretend . . . why you would dress like a . . . even if. . . ."

I stuck my finger into my drink and twirled the melting chips of ice. "There's more to it." I licked my finger. I would have to tell him the whole story. About my great-grandmother. About being a seventh daughter of a seventh daughter and trying to escape from that. About trying to outwit fate.

About Lucy.

Without looking at me, he listened to the voice he'd known as Ross's, telling what must have sounded like idiotic fairy tales. He said, "It's stupid to allow girls to grow up believing superstitious rubbish like that. It's going back to the dark ages."

"But it worked," I said.

"What worked?"

"I don't see patterns in things anymore." I smiled. I looked around briefly at the blades of grass, tree branches forming Y's, a wash of cloud streaking the sky. "I'm free."

"You say you inherited this – what? – talent from your great-grandmother?"

"It's more like a handicap."

"If this is true, suppose it was some other thing; for instance, a magnificent voice. Suppose you could imitate violins, a flute, shatter crystal with a high note. Quell wild beasts by speaking."

I waited, knowing what he was about to say.

"Do you think you could rid yourself of this talent by merely wishing it away, or pretending it didn't exist?"

"I could whisper. Or refuse to speak." I looked down at my sweating glass. I could see what he was getting at. Like my dark eyes. I could shut them, but they'd still be almost black beneath my eyelids.

"Maybe you just have a very vivid imagination."

I wanted to believe him – that I'd been mistaken about having a sixth sense, that I was as normal as anyone else.

"You have this imagination and maybe a fear as well – an unusual fear about the future, an anxiety. Maybe this is what caused you to think you could foretell things."

I told him about Mrs. Musgrove's tea leaves and the fortune she inherited.

He sat with his feet up on the chair, his bad foot tucked in, hugging his knees like a small boy. I did the same.

"Chance," he said.

I tried very hard to believe this. It was what Adele had said, yet coming from Adrian, it meant more.

"Yes," he said. He put his feet down and sat forward, earnestly. "You have a great desire to act, you see? You were asked to play the part of a fortune-teller, so you did. And you said the first thing that came into your head. Who wouldn't? People always hope the future will bring them money. Fortune-tellers read palms and tell people how long they're going to live and whether they'll receive money and –"

"Whether they'll fall in love," I supplied. Our eyes met briefly, but he looked away.

He continued, "So you see, it all fits together, in a way. It can be explained rationally. Your ability to see something in a pattern didn't go away because it never existed in the first place. Do you see what I mean?"

Looking into his eyes, again, I nodded, smiled, let a happy sigh escape. I could see whatever he wanted me to see.

"I just don't understand your family," he said. "Why would they let you pretend to be a boy? And other people. Didn't they think it was a bit . . . bizarre?"

"Sure. But they humor me. They think I'm slightly nuts, anyway. Maybe I am."

He looked at me, startled. "I don't think so," he said, with a hint of a smile. "But you certainly are different."

All the way home, I memorized his half-smile. "But you certainly are different," I told myself, puffing up hills, coasting down. "Certainly different." Certainly different and I love you. I tried that out a few times, but not out loud.

CHAPTER

15

Adrian came back to us to finish the lessons he had planned. I wore a sundress bought by Adele at Simpson's in Toronto. In a frenzy of relief at my return to girlhood, she had gone a little overboard at the end of her stay with Bea. "It reveals rather more of you than is quite seemly, but there it is, bought and paid for. Nothing I can do about it now." Her eyes rested approvingly on me, and I basked in that. She had me looking more or less the way she wanted me, I think, apart from my scarecrow hair. She asked no questions about what lay behind my return to normal. I guess she believed it to be bound up with the time of the month. I didn't think it was necessary to tell her I'd made a mistake, that Adrian believed that I didn't have second sight, that it was all coincidence and the result of an over-active imagination. If this was what Adrian believed, then I believed it, too.

I whumped myself down on the chair at the end of the garden, placed a foot across my knee as I used to do, and then thought better of it. Corny's eyes were on me as I fussed with my skirt, covering myself, trying to get comfortable. He examined my dress, which left my arms and shoulders bare, angling himself to get a peek down the front at the cleft between my breasts. I turned away from him, leaning on one elbow, looking up into Adrian's eyes as he discussed thermo-dynamics. It sounded like love poetry.

When he left to go back to university, I felt sick again. I ached for love; I wept from loneliness. Adele made me rest in bed most of the day. She bought me paints and canvases, and when she was satisfied that I had not had a relapse of scarlet fever, she let me spend the afternoons painting.

Corny went back to the farm, ready to enter high school. I refused to go. I couldn't face my old classmates after all I had been through in grade eight. Surprisingly, Adele agreed.

A friend of hers told her about a correspondence course that would be just right for me and so I stayed at home, studying in the morning, painting in the afternoon, and trying to stay in Adele's good graces. Pretending to be a boy had been childish; I could see that now. It hadn't accom-plished anything.

Trains carrying troops went through Kempton Mills reg-ularly, bound for Halifax and the Atlantic. I awoke in the night listening. Afternoons, I would look up from my paint-ing, waiting, hearing the engine's parting wail – a mournful *fa-re-th-ee-e-we-l-l-l.*

We planned Vanessa's wedding. Adele got out the list of

wedding guests from Beatrice's, adding some, subtracting others. Lists of things to do multiplied.

My mind was filled with Adrian. I worked with Red Cross workers, packing hampers with ration kits and warm socks, tobacco and mittens, chewing gum and knitted toques. "You're daydreaming again," our Red Cross leader often teased. We loaded the hampers into cars and took them down to the station to be piled onto a troop train for eventual shipment overseas. I watched trains chug into the station, watched the waving soldiers' eager faces peer from coach windows, grinning. Often my heart did flips. I kept seeing young men who almost looked like Adrian.

Painting kept me occupied. I did study after study of glass bottles, ceramic jars, dried flowers, bowls of fruit, using barely enough paint to cover the canvas. I avoided anything intricate, anything absorbing, anything in which a pattern might emerge. I kept my work lucid and light as dust.

The wedding was nearly upon us. Bea came home early with baby William to help get the house ready for the reception. Our bridesmaids' dresses were nearly finished and we needed only a final fitting.

The morning before the wedding, one of our cousins came to help Adele make sandwiches. She brought her two horrid children along. "Rosalind will be only too happy to keep them entertained," Adele said, smiling innocently at me.

We sat on the floor of the sitting room. "Shall we play Dominoes?" I asked.

Big scowls. They shook their heads.

"Parcheesi?"

"Hate Parcheesi!"

"Snakes and Ladders? Tiddlywinks? Murder?"

They grunted their boredom and shook their heads.

Noticing the trouble I was having with them, Marietta said firmly, "All right, we're going to play Pick-up Sticks." She got the game out of the cabinet, sat on the floor with us, gathered the sticks into a bunch, and let them go. The two kids were suddenly meek in Marietta's presence and took their turns, while I looked at the random scattering of sticks. "Your turn, Ros," Marietta said. She was sprawled on the floor like a child.

I stared at the colored sticks. Some of the yellow ones were far enough away from the others that I could easily pick one up without disturbing the pile. In fact, a ten-point red leaned on top at such an easy angle that, if I pressed on one end, I could take it. I saw this immediately, even as I felt my temperature rise and beads of sweat glaze my forehead.

"Feel free to take all day," Marietta said, lying back now with her arms behind her head, pretending to snore. The children giggled and imitated her.

Sweat stung my armpits, trickled down my ribs. My head pounded. I could hear nothing except a rush, like steam in a boiling kettle. I saw Marietta raise her head to look at me, lifting her arms with it, still folded behind her head, her elbows sticking out at the sides like wings. I saw her mouth form a question, her eyes change from a teasing impatience to sudden anxiety, and then saw her in dark outline – like an incomplete crayon drawing. I sensed rather than saw the children scrambling away, their mouths open. I felt Marietta take me by the shoulders, try to hold me close.

When I was able to see clearly, I heard an echo of my own voice shrieking about disaster, death, wailing Marietta's name. I pressed against her then, gripping her tightly. Marietta stroked my hair. Nearby, I glimpsed the frightened children. My high-pitched wail went on and on. The pick-up sticks lay broken and scattered all over the floor – the wreckage of Marietta's pattern of sticks. I had trampled them.

Adele and Bea ran into the room while I was still shrieking. "Control yourself, Rosalind!" Adele said. "You're all wrought up and overtired. The best place for you is bed. Off you go, now. Take an aspirin."

My head was splitting. I lay on my bed shivering, not sure what I had seen in the pattern of sticks, remembering only that I had to destroy it, as if I was also destroying death. I slept. Someone must have come in and covered me. I stayed in bed until late afternoon. When I came down, everyone asked how I was.

"Do you feel better?" Adele asked. "You must be hungry." No one mentioned my fit. It was as if nothing very much had happened.

Marietta said, "Smile, dahling; I'm still alive and kicking. You can't get rid of me that easily."

My sisters were all home, now, and kept me busy. That evening we cut flowers and arranged them in vases. The next morning we arranged tiny sandwiches on elegant plates. We got out the fruitcake Adele had made herself, arranged it in tiers, made icing, and iced it. The harder I worked and the more I chatted, the farther removed my premonition felt. I began to wonder if it had really been as bad as it seemed. Everyone's mind was on the wedding, trying to make it as beautiful as possible. And so was mine.

It was a promising day for a wedding – clouds in the morning, clearing by noon. The church was three-quarters full, many of the women in last year's hats, many of the young men in uniform.

One behind the other, my sisters and I floated up the center aisle in our pink satiny dresses and flowered headbands. Mine kept tipping forward, with so little hair to keep it in place. I was wearing high-heeled shoes for the first time. They made me wobble, but after those blasted boots of Corny's, they felt as delicate as glass slippers. I should have been con-centrating on the spacing. Instead, I let my eyes drift toward the guests. Dalton and wee William sat at the front with Adele. Adrian was two rows behind. It was Marietta who'd insisted he be sent an invitation. Inwardly, I had applauded.

I took in Corny, all neck and wrists but proud in a new suit. There was a faint dark line on his upper lip, as if he was growing a mustache. He winked at me, throwing my pacing off. I was in danger of treading on Cynthia, who had bunched herself up close to Sylvia. *Mustaches,* I thought. *What next?*

The twins and Bea and I arranged ourselves daintily near the altar and watched the others.

Marietta, the maid of honor, smiling as if she were the bride, large-boned and competent, loped toward the front of the church. Vanessa, on the arm of Uncle John, was radiant, if a little sharp-eyed. "This is to be a flawless wedding," she had warned all of us that morning. "No bungling, no tripping, no fits." She'd looked at me. "And no unseemly changes of gender."

Adele and my sisters had laughed. Marietta poked me in the ribs. "Cheer up," she said. "Don't take things so seriously." I tried smiling, and after a while I could.

Because of wartime shortages, the reception following the wedding ceremony was not lavish, but tasteful. Adele made sure of that. There was champagne, of course, as there had been at Beatrice's wedding. "Raspberry punch for the children," Adele said to me, but I pretended not to hear her.

My hair had grown a little, although it was still pretty short. Cynthia had curled it. I took off the stupid headband because I thought I looked more mature without it.

Soon the reception was in full swing. I stood alone for a moment, at the outer edge of the sitting room, leaning against the French door. Watching guests on the veranda, I listened to scattered bits of conversation.

"Adele's been lucky, on the whole, with the sons-in-law," I heard.

"Oh, indeed. Both solid young men."

"Give the family some stability."

"The youngest girl needs settling."

I glared over my shoulder and a portly gentleman, catching my glance, cleared his throat. The man with his back to me continued, "They won't find a man for her in a hurry."

His wife, sallow in faded mauve, added, "Adele's spoiled her, of course, letting her go so queer that time. Pretending to be a boy. Never heard of such goings-on in all my life. Isn't there another child put away somewhere? Off her head, I think I once heard. Must run in the family."

I shifted my attention. Near the dining room arch, Adrian was deep in conversation with Marietta. Something she said made him smile, then laugh. He took her elbow and steered her toward the French doors, but before they had moved very far, they were caught up in a cluster of people. Adrian seemed to have grown, or filled out a bit. He glanced my way, and I smiled. We had not had a chance to speak except very briefly during the receiving line. The best man was making his way toward Marietta. He put an arm around her shoulders and removed her from the circle. "One more photograph," I heard him say.

Adrian angled through the guests toward me. He studied me for a moment, biting his lip, as if he might be addressing the wrong person, or might use the wrong name. "I think you would have trouble getting away with your act now," he said quietly.

I looked away. "Wasn't it a nice wedding?" I said.

He finished off his champagne. "The Kemp girls looked stunning." He had been standing at a little distance from me, but was forced closer to allow someone to pass behind. He was looking at me with frank curiosity. I gazed back for several heartbeats before I looked away.

"Sorry if I keep staring," he said, "I'm still having trouble adjusting to you." A maid hired for the occasion offered him fresh champagne. I took one, too. He frowned at me.

"I'm allowed," I lied.

We took our glasses outside, where it was cooler and quieter, and made our way around to the back garden. Others were standing in intimate clusters, with small plates of dainty refreshments. I followed as Adrian made his way toward some men talking to a tall luscious young woman who made me think of sponge cake with mounds and swirls of boiled icing. Her name was Alice. She was as tall as Adrian, and smiled down at me as if I were someone's little sister. Well I was, but still, I was wearing grown-up high heels and silk stockings.

While they talked over my head, I felt childishly beneath notice. Alice moved closer, offering Adrian a tiny sandwich from her plate, forcing me to take a step back. I was apparently invisible. I noticed Adrian's gaze stray to Alice's deep neckline.

Corny galloped energetically toward us, camera at the ready. Trying to keep his back to the sun, he urged people to move closer and say cheese. Marietta strode across the grass to our group, with two plates and a hopeful smile. "Hold still for a moment," Corny called to her. "I don't have one of the maid of honor."

She stopped, still smiling, squinting into the sun while he snapped her picture. Her smile seemed to be for the camera, but she was looking at Adrian. She handed him a plate of tiny triangular sandwiches.

Several young men in uniform joined the group and the chatter turned to war talk. I tried to tune out the conversation and fill my mind with other things – robins calling for rain, a breeze carrying off someone's hat. I was able to obscure the words, but was still aware of the shape of sounds. The men's voices boomed out promises, threats, laughter. There was the staccato, rapid-fire listing of facts, of place-names, of victories. A rumbling murmur of defeats. I moved as inconspicuously as possible away from the voices and slipped through the gap in the fence into the much overgrown thicket.

Near the climbing tree, I stopped to put my champagne glass down on the flat surface of a large rock and heard the rustle of someone pushing aside branches along the path. My shoes were pinching my feet and I longed to take them off.

Adrian came into sight and stood still, hands dangling at his sides. "I was afraid you might be. . . ." He stopped. I wondered if he thought I was embarking on another transformation. "I thought the champagne might have made you . . . might have upset you."

"I'm not a child," I said glumly. "I'm nearly fourteen." I

sat on the rock beside my empty glass, my dress ballooning rosily around me.

"I know," he said, as if humoring a child. He reached for my hand. "Come. You'll spoil your dress."

He helped me to my feet and released my hand. We ambled toward the pond, both of us limping. I stopped and hung on to his arm while I took off my shoes. He looked startled. "Don't worry," I said, "I'm not about to strip down to my bare essentials."

He smiled wryly, his neck and ears slightly pink. He seemed awkward now, talking quickly, asking questions, asking about my painting, my correspondence courses. I asked about his studies at university. I said, "We could write to each other, you know."

"I'd never know whether to address a letter to Dear Rosalind or Dear Ross."

"Don't."

"I'm only teasing."

"I can take it from other people, but not from you."

He had his arms folded, one fist propping his chin, studying me, frowning. "What makes *me* so different?"

I looked at my feet; I'd put a hole in my precious silk stocking. I wanted to say something memorable. I wanted to capture him with murmurs of love. Instead, point-blank, I croaked, "Do you like me?"

He stood still, wide-eyed, his mouth open. "Like you? Of course I like you. How could you think otherwise?" He smiled.

I held him with my eyes, wanting to bewitch him. He became serious, gazing back, seeing, it seemed, my eyes and nothing else. I willed him closer, watching him become drawn in, enchanted. I wanted him to kiss me.

A tree branch snapped. *"Ouch!"* Corny's voice. He came into view, Marietta behind him. Adrian looked around, like a man suddenly shaken awake.

My heart was pounding, my lips parted. I staggered back a step, thinking that this was what it might be like to die of starvation.

We stood looking awkwardly at one another. Marietta turned visibly pale, as if a light had gone out, stealing her color. Corny looked bitterly from Adrian to me and back, as if he'd been stabbed by his best friend. He raised his camera. "Watch the birdie," he said gruffly.

Marietta told us that the speeches were starting, but it didn't sound like her voice. I caught her bleak look of resignation as she turned, walking at first, then running, back to the garden. I began to run after her, but turned to get Adrian, pulling him by the arm, pulling him with me. I wanted to take him and give him to Marietta. Push him toward her. But Marietta was out of sight and Adrian stumbled.

Adrian hurried across the garden toward the guests gathered near the back porch. Corny was nowhere to be seen.

I couldn't get close to Marietta. There were too many people between us. I started to call her, but the toasts had begun, and the minister's wife frowned at me and put her finger to her lips. I stood still, in my stockinged feet, anxiously clutching my shoe straps. I tried to concentrate on the best man talking about Vanessa, and what a fine young woman she was, and Uncle John talking about her new husband, and how lucky he was to be marrying into such a distinguished family.

After an eternity, the speeches were over. I hadn't taken my eyes off Marietta. Before the guests could disperse, she put her fingers in her mouth, and with an unladylike but piercing whistle, got everyone's attention. I saw Adele wince.

Marietta climbed the steps of the back porch and looked merrily out over the guests assembled in the garden. "I have something to announce," she said. "I apologize to Vanessa and Jack for cashing in on the excitement, but I want to tell everyone before I change my mind again. After vacillating for months now, I've finally made a decision. I'm going overseas!" She took a sip of champagne, swaying slightly, smiling into the faces of friends and relatives, who were momentarily stunned into silence. They buzzed to life with a barrage of questions. I squeezed through the press of guests toward her.

"With the Army Medical Corps," I heard her reply. "Oh, I *have* been training. I just didn't want to tell my family until I'd decided for sure."

Adele sat down suddenly in a garden chair and began fanning her face. "I knew it! I was afraid this would happen. You should have warned us," she said, tearfully. "You should at least have given us a hint."

"And what would you have said?" Marietta asked boldly, coming down and taking Adele's hand.

"I'd have told you not to be so foolish." Adele patted her chest to slow the beating of her heart.

"When will you go?" Beatrice wanted to know. "Not immediately, I hope."

"Soon," Marietta chirped. "I'm pretty sure I'll be with the Fifth General Hospital at Cliveden – the estate of Lord Astor, no less." She was being very jolly.

Uncle John came up beside her and said loudly, "Let's have three cheers for our little lady doctor!"

Everyone obliged, except me. My head was humming. I skirted the group surrounding Marietta, maneuvered myself up the porch steps, through the door, and up the back stairs as the noise in my head began to change to a roar. In the bathroom, I vomited.

Later, they all said it was the heat, the excitement. "The champagne!" Adele said. Marietta sat on the side of my bed. All the guests had gone long ago. "Don't take it so hard."

I turned away. "Don't go."

"But I want to go. For once in my life I can do something useful, something really stupendous."

"It's my fault. It's because of . . . Adrian."

"Adrian be damned. You're a goose of a girl to think Adrian means anything in that way. You know me. I just want some live action. I want a swell time."

"I can't let you go. It's my fault."

"You can't stop me, and nothing's your fault. How much power do you think you have?"

This was what was beginning to worry me. I didn't know. Again, I saw Adrian's eyes. It was as if, at that moment, I had had the power to enchant him.

Much worse, though, was the memory of the pick-up sticks. I had had the most powerful feeling that something bad was going to happen. It had filled my head with something I could barely describe – shattering, deafening, benumbing chaos.

"I'll be just fine. Anyway, what can you do about it?" She prodded me, trying to get me to look at her. "Listen, it's my life, and I'm in charge of it. So stop worrying about events beyond your control."

I said, resignedly, "There are two hundred and fifteen individual objects, counting books and hair curlers, on that side of the room alone. I've taken up counting things."

"What on earth for?"

"To push bad thoughts out of my brain."

She patted my head and told me to go to sleep.

16

Marietta sailed for Britain shortly after Vanessa's wedding, and as autumn turned into winter, I kept myself busy with studying and painting. I was trying to do a portrait of Marietta from memory.

Her first letter home was filled with awe and excitement: *I'm really here. I can scarcely believe it. In the back of my mind, I must admit that I only half-believed in the reality of Britain and half-suspected it was a figment of the novelists' imaginations. In spite of the destruction, in spite of the grimness and the uniforms and the injuries, it really exists. The people look so different from us. They sound different, of course, and their houses (those left untouched by the bombs), their streets, policemen, stores, telephones, everything is so enchantingly British. I anticipate each new day as if I am the heroine of an adventure. I have traveled to another world. I'm in love with life.*

Adele had sent a package of good-quality, white, cotton, Canadian-made underwear, enough for each day of the week. Marietta wrote back that if she was blown to bits by a bomb, at least the family would have the comfort of knowing she was wearing decent underwear, clean and made in Canada.

Corny sent me some of the snapshots he'd taken at Vanessa's wedding. One of them, slightly blurred, was of a startled Adrian, and me looking moony and lovesick. I put it between the slightly rain-warped pages of *Emile*, on a shelf at the back of my closet. A little shrine.

In early December the headaches began, accompanied by a strange sound, like a dull needle rasping over the end of a well-worn record. Adele wanted me to go to Dr. Harmon, but I refused. "He will think I'm more of a fruitcake than he does already." One night I screamed in my sleep and woke Adele and the twins. "Something has happened," I sobbed, when they all came into my room.

"*Shhh,* it's all right," Adele tried to soothe. "It was only a bad dream."

Two days later a cablegram came from overseas to Adele, saying that Marietta had been injured in a bombing raid. She phoned Beatrice and Vanessa; she phoned Lydia and John. She talked endlessly about each word of the message and what it might mean, how badly she might be injured. She wondered over and over if they might send Marietta home. The more she talked, the stronger her voice became, and the more she sounded as though she could handle anything.

I was desolate. Talking was out of the question. I could not paint or read, much less do my lessons. Instead, I talked to myself: "The cable said injured, not dead. Your nightmare was pure coincidence. People are going to get hurt in a war. No one can predict when or where."

Or can they?

On and on I went, saying words, not believing them, trying to count objects, not getting past twenty.

Soon letters came, which Adele passed along to all of us, first from a friend, a nurse, writing at Marietta's request. The friend explained that Marietta had been granted a short leave after a hectic few weeks of heavy bombing. *We were all worked practically to death,* she wrote. *Marietta, especially. She always seemed to make time for one more task. She deserved that leave, let me tell you. She took it with several others, including her close friend and colleague Captain David Mills. Their aim was to visit some out-of-the-way place where they could forget the war for a day or two. They were heading for the Cotswolds, I believe, when the inn where they spent their first night was bombed and Captain Mills was killed. Marietta asked me to give you these few details as she is emotionally unable to herself.*

Soon a letter came from Marietta. We were not to worry about her; she was fine, recovering, a few broken ribs, a burn. Nothing to lose sleep over. *I am in a convalescent hospital, where they seem to have more sun than the rest of England put together. I'm feeling deliciously spoiled. I'm ready to go back to work, but THEY say I need a rest.* I detected a false heartiness.

She wrote a postscript to me: *I'M FINE! SEE! They won't get rid of me with a few bombs. A steamroller, perhaps, or a locomotive, possibly. THEY may send me home for a month. Won't that be jolly?*

Marietta arrived in Kempton Mills just before Christmas, and would not be sailing from Halifax again until the middle of January. Our family would be together for the holidays.

On a blustery afternoon, Beatrice and Dalton arrived with their baby. Vanessa and Jack arrived Christmas Eve afternoon. The tall Christmas tree, drooping with painted glass orbs and scepters, listed threateningly. "I'll fix it," Jack offered. He waded through a sea of tissue-wrapped presents to tie it to the radiator, causing spruce needles to rain on everything.

The smell of shortbread and mincemeat pies filled every corner of the house. Adele had been hoarding the rationed sugar to use all at once.

The healing burns on Marietta's shoulder and neck, which she dressed herself, were almost completely covered by her clothes. Her fractured ribs and collarbone had pretty well mended. She was supposed to keep her right arm in a sling, but had to be reminded. Her eyes tore at my heart. They were too bright, glistening, as if tears were held in check only by the strength of her determined smile. A face of porcelain.

Marietta and I went downtown late that afternoon for some last-minute shopping. Snow fell on our shoulders and noses. We followed the man with the horse-drawn snowplow clearing a path down Hill Street just before dark. Snow squeaked underfoot. Head back, I caught snowflakes on my tongue. Marietta saved me from stepping in a neat pile of horse droppings, soon to become frozen road apples.

"*Ew!* Could you imagine?"

"Once you picked one up," Marietta said.

"Oh, I never did."

"And threw it at me."

"I did not. Did I get you?"

Her laughter reminded me of the recorded laughter in the Fun House at the Exhibition.

In front of the stores, men, too old to go overseas, shoveled snow from the sidewalk into mountains. They shooed away kids who got in their way trying to climb them and slide down. The streetlights came on.

I made Marietta stop to look in the jewelry shop window at mechanical skaters in bonnets and capes, twirling on mirrored ice to a tinny *Skaters' Waltz* piped out to the street. Over and over they cut the same circles, made the same turns with the same partners in the same top hats, reflected endlessly inside a mirrored, open-fronted box. I watched, fascinated, and then caught Marietta's reflection. Unsmiling, she gazed, glassy-eyed, at something else – perhaps a scene two thousand miles from the jeweler's window. When we moved on, she tightened her smile muscles again, causing an ache in my throat.

Wee William's little stocking hung from the fireplace. After everyone else had gone to bed, I felt I had enough nerve to ask Marietta about David Mills.

"David? Oh, he was wonderful! You'd have liked him. He wasn't all that good-looking . . . well, he was sort of good-looking. He was wiry, athletic, really. He had the most endearing feet. They turned out slightly when he walked. Reminded me a bit of a duck."

I laughed. "So far, I'm enchanted."

"But his smile," she said, "it would have melted the iceberg that sank the *Titanic*. He had nurses, orderlies, patients, fellow doctors, eating out of his hand. Just with that little smile, the little curve, that soft glow in his eyes." She smiled now, remembering. "Well, not just his smile, I mean, along with his smile went a personality. Everyone liked him."

Neither of us spoke for a moment. The clock in the hall groaned toward a chime, but didn't achieve it. It was only the quarter hour. Marietta was swallowing hard, face averted, eyelids trying to brace against a flood. I thought I could hear her heart, but it was my own. I knelt at her feet and put my arms around her. She bent over me, her silent tears washing my pale head. No sound. An intake of breath, finally. Then small releases. An outpouring.

We celebrated Christmas, going through the ritual opening of presents one at a time so that everyone could see and everyone be thanked. Wee William's favorite gift was the orange he found in the toe of his stocking. Aunt Lydia, Uncle John, and Corny joined us for the day and helped eat the immense turkey Adele had managed to get.

Adrian paid a call New Years' Day, before going back to university. He had a car now, and came over partly to show it off and partly to see Marietta. He and Marietta chatted in their old friendly manner. "I was sorry to hear about your loss," he said.

She patted his hands and thanked him, eyes downcast.

I was remembering how I had tried to give Adrian to her at Vanessa's wedding, wanting to thrust him right into her arms. *As if I had the power to do that!*

Adrian asked when she was going back. "If I'm home that weekend, I'll come and say good-bye."

Marietta smiled at him then, and I had to turn away for fear that my jealousy would show. I hadn't even the power to control that.

Marietta's leave was running out. Bea and little William came back a few days before her departure, and so did Vanessa. Marietta would catch the early-evening passenger train on Sunday bound for Ottawa, and on Monday take a troop train heading for Halifax to sail for Europe.

One night at dinner, Marietta said, "David's sister lives not too far from here, in Arnprior. I'd phone her if I had the nerve."

"Why nerve?" Vanessa asked.

"Because I'm not sure whether David wrote to her about us." She was able to talk about him now without stopping to swallow her tears. "In another time, another place, we would have been planning our wedding," she said.

It was Adele's turn to have tears in her eyes. Her expression tender, she nodded sadly. It was clear that Marietta was a great credit to her.

We all helped with the dishes after dinner while Adele kept the baby amused. She told us to change the dishwater when it got too greasy, and to dry things carefully before putting them away. This last request was directed at Marietta, who was drying two plates at a time, shuffling them like cards.

Bea said, "Marietta, I think you should phone David's sister."

"But, what if she says, 'Marietta who?'"

"She won't. Don't put it off any longer. Just go and do it."

We were at the pots and pans stage of the dishes by the time Marietta came back out to the kitchen, glowing. "She's just like him," she said, "same expressions, same sense of humor. We both cried and then laughed and then cried again and sounded like idiots and she knew all about me. David wrote to her and her husband ages ago. Ages ago!" Marietta's eyes drifted back into a past invisible to the rest of us. "I'm going to visit them tomorrow and spend the night." She looked at Adele. "I'll take the train from Arnprior straight through to Ottawa."

Adele was about to complain, but stopped herself. She looked back at this headstrong woman, once her little girl, and nodded, shoulders sagging. Poor Adele. Her control over us was slowly seeping away. She turned her attention to her small grandson, busily taking canned goods out of a cupboard.

Watching Marietta pick up a handful of cutlery from the drainer, I was transfixed by the knives, forks, and spoons rattling onto the table as she carelessly dried them. Suddenly my head began to pound, as if it would explode. Without warning, blood rushed from my nose, splattering my tea towel, the front of my dress, the table, the silver flatware as it lay skewed every which way. Marietta stared, immobilized. Beatrice swooped down and gathered up her baby. Vanessa turned from the dishpan and yelled, "For Pete's sake, Ros!" The twins covered their faces.

"Lean over the sink!" Adele commanded.

"But the dishwater!" Vanessa yelped.

I held the tea towel to my nose, leaned my head back against the wall, and concentrated. Soon the nosebleed stopped and everyone calmed down.

"You'd better go up to bed," Adele said to me. "You've obviously had too much excitement."

I went upstairs and soon fell into a fitful sleep, dreaming about struggling through a molasses-like atmosphere to prevent some unknown disaster.

*

The next day, following breakfast, one by one we all drifted up to Marietta's room, leaning against her door frame, against the windowsill, sitting on her bed, watching her pack her suitcase.

"I don't understand," Cynthia said to her. "Why are you visiting these people? I mean, you don't even know them."

Sylvia said, "Cynth-i-aw, must you be completely dense?"

"Honestly!" Cynthia left the room.

"I don't like the way you're just heaving everything into that suitcase," Adele fretted. "Fold things."

A glimpse in Marietta's mirror showed my reflection – sad-eyed, pinched about the lips. I moved out of range. I wanted to say, "Don't go," but couldn't think of a reason.

Vanessa said, "It will be awkward staying with total strangers, don't you think?" Adele frowned at her.

"They aren't *total* strangers." Marietta closed her bag. She turned and took a long look at me. "What's the matter with you, with that long face?"

"Nothing. I just . . . don't go."

"I have to go sooner or later. What difference can twenty-four hours make?" I concentrated on the toes of my shoes. I could scarcely hear her for the rush of sound in my ears. "Listen," Marietta said, "when the train goes through Kempton Mills tomorrow night, come down and wave to me. Maybe it will pause long enough for me to get off for a few minutes."

We all drove to the station with her (except Bea, who was putting the baby down for a nap) and had the usual

Kemp family farewell dragged out with hugs and last-minute reminders to be careful, to write, to not work so hard; and promises and don't forgets and hugs all around again. Adele gave her a tin of cookies to take for her hostess. She boarded the train for Arnprior seconds before it pulled away from the station.

Sunday was dull, with a damp mist signaling that either rain or wet snow was on the way. Restlessly I paced the house, unable to read, or paint, or even sit on the floor and play roly-poly with the baby. After lunch I bundled up and went outside into the woodlot. There wasn't much snow, and what there was, was flecked with black from the trees. I skirted the pond, with its thin layers of gray ice around the edges. In a moment I found myself beside the tree where I had stashed Faye Wirt's barrette. I reached into the hole. My fingers closed around the barrette, and as I pulled it out, my head began to pound. I put the barrette in my pocket this time and hurried back to the house, my feet keeping time with the pounding in my head that, once again, sounded like feet running.

Not knowing she'd already left, Adrian arrived in the afternoon to say good-bye to Marietta. "I didn't realize how bad the weather was until after I'd set out from Oxford Landing," he said. "The snow has turned to sleet. There's a sheet of ice covering everything."

Adele said, "I don't think you should think of driving anywhere until this weather clears." He looked a little sheepish, but agreed to come in and wait out the weather. "Now you'll stay for dinner," Adele said. It was more an order than an invitation. "Marietta's train comes through town at seven thirty and, weather permitting, the girls will go down to the station to wave. I'll stay here with the baby."

"Oh," he said. "All right." He glanced sideways at me and shrugged, as if he realized he was being held captive. "Thank you."

My mood brightened considerably. Vanessa got out a deck of cards and we all played rummy until it was time to set the table. I could scarcely take my eyes off Adrian. A few times he looked over at me and smiled, which made me blush. At dinner he sat beside me. I ate almost nothing. All I could think about were his hands, the hair on the back of his wrists, the very heat from his body so close to me. I wasn't even aware of time passing, of Vanessa phoning the station, of her saying the train was going to be late.

Instead of helping with the dishes, I went outside to help Adrian put chains on the tires of his car to prevent it skidding on the ice. Mostly I stood shivering and admiring his back, his legs, his head, even his deformed foot in its built-up shoe, while he did all the work. He had just got the chains in place when my sisters came running out, putting on their coats. Adele, the baby in her arms, closed the door behind them.

"The train's already in the station," Vanessa shouted. "We'd better hurry if we're going to see her." She nearly slipped on the bottom step. The others sideslipped to the car and got in.

I stood in the driveway as if frozen. It was happening again – the noise, the pounding, lights, chaos. "Rosalind, get in," I heard. And then someone – Bea, I think – yanked me into the car beside her.

"Something's going to happen!" I shrieked. I was in tears.

There were soothing noises, hands pressing, calming.

"Nothing's going to happen."

I was aware of pressure inside my head and was afraid I might have another nosebleed. Adrian's car crept through the fog. I wasn't conscious of making any sound, but my sisters told me to stop, to stop moaning. It was getting on everyone's nerves. I thought I *had* stopped until Vanessa yelled, "For Pete's sake, Ros, shut up!"

We saw the station lights. Marietta's train – passenger train 550, eastbound – stood at the station. For the past little while, apparently, the fireman had been stoking the boiler, trying to get up enough steam to drive the "cantankerous old hog" (as he later described the engine) to Carleton Place and then on to Ottawa. It had set out from Petawawa, in the upper Ottawa Valley, right on time, but had gradually slowed down due to the severe weather. It had reached Pembroke, moved slowly to Cobden and Renfrew, laboring on to Arnprior, and finally to Kempton Mills, losing time at every stop.

Coach lights revealed that it was packed; passengers stood in the aisles. Outside, a few people milled under the overhang of the station roof, waiting to wave relatives off.

I opened the car door before Adrian had pulled to a stop in the parking area. My sisters shrieked at me, and Bea pulled me back. I was still crying. "We have to get her off the train," I pleaded. I tore free and got out of the car. "MARIETTA!"

I screamed. People turned to look. Ahead of me, a girl running to get on the train turned and fell in my path. "No!" I shouted at her. "Don't get on!" When she tried to get up, I pushed her down.

"I have to! My father!"

A man shot past not seeing us and jumped onto the train. "Boar-r-rd!" the conductor cried.

Leaving the girl, I ran toward the train. "WAIT!" I screamed at the conductor. "GET THEM OFF!" I slipped on the ice and fell. Someone tried to help me up, but I crawled out of reach and stumbled to my feet.

Too late. The conductor had ushered the last straggler up into the coach and had himself boarded the train. I could see him through the coach window reach up to pull the signal cord to tell the engineer to start.

I heard the steam whistle of the troop train approaching from the west seconds before I saw its headlight through the fog spotlighting the last couple of wooden coaches of the passenger train. Heads turned, mouths gaped, disbelieving.

"She's comin' in too fast!" someone yelled. Bystanders, as if swept by a wave, moved back toward the parked cars. Someone grasped me around the waist, dragging me with the crowd.

"Nobody musta signaled them!"

"God in heaven!"

"Holy Moses!"

Sound of splintering wood. Pick-up sticks flung into the air to fall as they might. Bodies tossed up to fall at a fixed rate of speed. The massive locomotive pulling a troop train from Red Deer, Alberta, tore through the last two coaches of the evening local like the prow of a ship parting the waves. It tossed their roofs up and wooden sides out like so much foam, grinding to a halt, bearing the debris of undercarriages in front of it.

I thought my brain had stopped, and my heart.

CHAPTER

17

"Why?" Adele asked over and over, shaking her head, looking heavenward, tears streaming down her face. No one answered. No one could.

After the shattering, mind-numbing collision, after the blackness and bleakness of the funeral, my next unfogged memory was of Adrian sitting with me, trying to get me to listen to him, or to at least look at him, as I sat staring into the fire in the grate.

"Whether or not you are clairvoyant," he said, "it was not your fault."

"I know," I said. But I thought, *Yes it was.* If I hadn't been so lovesick for Adrian, I might have been able to pay more attention to the signals; I could have said to Marietta. . . .

"Nothing you could have said to Marietta would have prevented her from being on that train."

"I know."

"You cannot control fate. If you tell people that they are headed for disaster, they won't listen." He said, "Marietta died because she was in the wrong place at the wrong time. *She* chose her path, not you. If you are guilty of anything, it is in believing that you hold destiny in your hands."

"I know." But, I thought, *I could have held on to her and never let her go.*

"You saved someone's life, you know. You held on to a young girl and prevented her from getting on the train."

"I did?" I frowned. I had lost all memory of this. It had been swept away, like a dream I couldn't recall.

He stood up, looking at me sadly. "I have to go, but, I'd like to come again, if I may."

My heart should have leapt for joy. I would see him again. But, it just hung there inside my chest, pumping away. I nodded yes.

The *Kempton Mills Banner* described the accident as one of the worst in Canada. One hundred and fifty-eight were injured and thirty-six people died. Marietta was listed among them. So, too, was Joseph Wirt, Faye Wirt's father.

I was at home alone, about a week after the accident, when someone knocked on our side door. I had to force myself to answer it. Faye Wirt, looking almost grown-up, stood on our doorstep. Numbly, stupidly, I said, "No one's here. I mean, no one else."

"I came to see you," she said.

It took me a moment to understand. "Oh, would . . . would you like to come in?" I hoped she wouldn't.

"I guess so. For a minute."

I started to lead her into the sitting room, but she stopped where she was. "The kitchen's okay."

I shrugged. "Want to take off your coat?"

She shook her head. "I'm not staying very long. My sister's coming by to pick me up in about fifteen minutes." She looked at her watch, which for some reason made me look at mine. We both sat down at the kitchen table. "I came here to tell you, first of all, that I'm sorry about your sister." Tears sprang into my eyes. Miss Coombs had been right. Grief is a lonely state. No one can really share it. I looked down and blinked and mumbled a thank-you.

"No," she said, "it's me thanking you." I must have looked puzzled because she continued, "Thank you for holding me back from the train."

Now it all came clear – the girl who fell in front of me, my yelling not to get on the train, the man running past.

"I've been secretly living with my sister all this time," Faye said, "away from here, on a farm near Carleton Place." I nodded, knowing without really knowing. She went on, "I had to come back here to get something. I had left some money hidden in my room, and all the time I was away, I worried about it. I was afraid the old man would get it. Then we heard he was trying to sell the house. I just had to take the risk. I didn't tell my sister because she would have said no.

"I hitched a ride here that afternoon, figuring I could wait till the old man went out, use my key to get in, grab my money, and go back by train that night. But he caught me.

He knew I'd hid some money before I disappeared and he'd looked everywhere for it. He locked me in my room and said he'd kill me unless I told him where it was."

I was spellbound. For the first time since Marietta's death, I had something else to think about. "But – how did you get away?"

"I waited, and held off telling him anything, and all that time he was drinking, and while he was drinking, I snuck my money out of the hole in my bedroom wall, down behind my bed, and hid it inside my underwear. And by and by, when he was good and drunk, I told him the money was hidden down near the station. I knew he'd believe that about the station because I heard he found my boxcar down there and he killed my cat in it for revenge." Her eyes filled up when she told me this, and she had to stop for a minute.

"Would you like some ginger ale?" I asked her, but she shook her head and went on.

"He grabbed me, made me get in the car and drive to the station. I've been able to drive for a couple of years, now. So while I drove, he pressed a knife to the side of my neck. As soon as I parked and saw the train was in, I panicked. I was scared I wouldn't get away. I don't know what made me think of it, but I turned my head fast as a snake and bit his hand. Then I ran like blazes for the train, with him after me. That's when I fell and you held me down, and he was so plastered he didn't even notice, and now he's dead and it's what he deserved."

Faye's face was a lather of perspiration. I poured some ginger ale anyway and she drank it.

"Now that he's gone," I said, "do you think you and your sister will come back here to live?"

"No. Everyone treated us like dirt here, all on account of the old man. He was like a poison in our family, and Betty, my sister, knew it. She cleared out the first chance she got. Randy Norton took a shine to her, so she ran away with him and got married. He's a nice fellow and doing well with his farm. Betty always said she'd come and get me when she got the chance, and so she did. When the police asked her about me, she lied. Randy didn't mind having me there. He's a good farmer and a fair man."

"Did you know they scoured the whole area looking for you?"

"I suppose they would. Well, so what? First time anyone paid any attention to me in my whole life. No need to hide, now, I guess. I go by the name Norton, though – Faye Norton."

We heard a car horn. Faye looked through the window and got up to leave. "Well, the reason I came was to thank you, and I did, but I also should say sorry, sorry for being so mean to you at school."

I didn't know what to say, so I said, "Oh." Then I said, "I guess I used to wonder what I'd done to deserve it."

"Nothing. It wasn't you, it was your mother."

My eyebrows shot up.

"She used to bring us boxes of cast-off clothes from your sisters, sometimes toys, and quite often food. It was all good things and useful, and we fell on the food like we were starved, which half the time we were, and fought over the toys. What I hated most were the clothes. I had to wear your sisters' clothes to school and I was sure you were laughing about it behind my back and telling the other kids what a charity case I was. So sticking my ruler into you was the only way I could think of to get back at you."

"I never knew!" My voice sounded hollow.

"You didn't recognize the clothes?"

"No. I never really notice people's clothes."

"I'm sorry about it now," Faye said, "because now that I come to think about it, your mother is one of the kindest, most generous women in the whole town."

"She is? But, we didn't know."

"Well, there, you see? That's the way she is. Betty once wrote her a sort of thank-you note and she wrote back to say she didn't want to be thanked. For her it was something she needed to do – make herself useful. This is what she said: *If you can't find a way to be helpful, you might as well go to bed, turn your face to the wall, and wait for death.* Funny, I've always remembered that."

"Funny. You actually know her better than I do."

"Hardly. I sure thought I knew you, though. A brainy little twerp in your nice store-bought clothes, cute as a button with your big dark eyes and hair the color of straw. The opposite of me."

She opened the door to leave, and then came back in. She put out her hand. "Let's shake and be friends," she said. After the door closed, I stood there trying to remember everything she said, especially about my mother.

Days passed. Vanessa had long since gone back to Jack, Bea and the baby to Dalton. The twins went back to school, finally. Adele once again picked up her busy life.

Moping around my room one day, supposedly tidying it up, I came across the picture Lucy had drawn of me. I stared at it for a long time, thinking about her, about this skill she had. I might go back there someday. After all, she *is* my sister. And we *do* have drawing in common.

I began to see that the sun still shone. The snow glistened. Food had a little more flavor. I walked downtown by myself for the first time in months. People I knew nodded to me, said hello, asked how we were all getting along. I passed the tree whose growing roots bulged up, cracking the concrete. Through the barbershop window, I saw Vincent cutting a little boy's hair. Across the street, a woman coiffed and curled came out of Miss Edwards' beauty parlor.

I walked home by way of the high school and heard the last bell ring. Grown-up-looking boys and girls poured out in clusters, singly, in couples. I stood off to the side, watching them. A boy winked at me as he passed. I felt myself reddening. Soon Sylvia and Cynthia came out and we walked home together. *I could get used to going to high school*, I thought.

"Maybe I'll go back to school," I said.

Sylvia said, "You'll probably get teased about pretending to be a boy."

I thought about it. "After everything that's happened, teasing doesn't sound like a very big problem."

Cynthia said, "Are you going to tell anyone that you're, you know, clairvoyant?"

"Cynth-i-aw! Why bring that up?" Sylvia said.

"Well, why not bring it up?" I said. "It's a fact of life. My life. It's something I have to live with, whether I want to or not. It might even prove useful someday. But no, I won't tell anyone. Unless I make a friend. I would tell my best friend, if I had one."

We walked along, not saying much. Cynthia put an arm around my shoulders and gave me a quick squeeze. "Maybe I can see into the future a little bit, too," she said. "What I see is you having friends. Lots of them."

I grinned at her. Maybe she was right. After all, here I was deciding that I could live with myself the way I am. Who knows what other miracles might happen.

The End.